Death Beads: Guardian of the Dreamcatcher Series

By

Melinda Williams

Cover design by Katie Kamara

Soma Fusion Media LLC
3811 Suitland Rd SE
Washington. D.C. 20020
USA

somafusionmedia@gmail.com
www.somafusionmedia.com

Published by Soma Fusion Media LLC 2020

ISBN: (Digital) 978-1-63760-896-8
        (Print) 978-1-63760-897-5

Acknowledgements

I would like to thank

Katie Kamara

&

Soma Fusion Media LLC

for making this book a reality.

Chapter 1

"Dammit!" Tribal Officer Chase Spirit Walker slammed his foot on the brake of his police cruiser and skidded to a stop, a cloud of dust from the unpaved road swirling red in the reflection of his rearview mirror. He chuckled nervously at his overreaction as he watched a solitary tumbleweed whirl across the road, illuminated by the cruiser's headlights, before disappearing into the inky gloom. Maintaining his constant vigilance, not to mention uninterrupted sleep, was a chore thanks to the unsettling dreams that had plagued him since the first murder—dreams that had worsened each time a nearby rancher was found slain—ten in all, now. Every night since the first, he'd scoured the reservation in hopes of preventing more, intent on protecting his people from the evil spirit roaming their lands. Chase toyed with the dream catcher hanging around his neck. Why the recurring nightmares evaded the amulet's protection he didn't know, any more than he knew what the dreams of a shape-shifting twin brother meant.

"Focus, Chase. Focus." His voice sounded hollow in the empty confines of his car and he rubbed his eyes, blinking to re-adjust his vision to the darkness of the desolate surroundings.

He eased the car forward, scanning the deserted road—the same road he'd seen in his latest dream. He jerked his head to the left at a piercing howl. A solitary coyote sat sentinel beneath towering mesquite trees swaying in the murky night like skeletons. Chase caught a flash of gray fur and gold eyes before the sacred animal—known as the medicine dog to most Apaches—scurried into the trees. If folklore was to be believed—and Chase did believe—some kind of medicine, good or bad, was on its way. His soul understood the coyote's silent emptiness. The signs—both physical and spiritual—surrounded him.

Chase's eyes continued their quest for something, anything; he could take as a sign. He slammed on his brakes a second time when a large, winged bird swooped down from the sky and skimmed the hood of his cruiser. In one fluid moment, Chase threw open the door and bolted from the car. Hands on his hips, he scanned the black sky from treetop to treetop.

There! Perched on an overhead branch, the great horned owl's yellow eyes fixed on his own. He leaned against his patrol unit as his stomach clenched. The Apache omen of death.

Satisfied he'd delivered his warning, the bird's wingtip skimmed his window and soared over the car circling Coyote Canyon.

Chase turned to climb into his patrol unit; a moan from the dry wash raised the hairs on the back of his neck. Something was out there—something or someone. He reached into his patrol unit, retrieved a flashlight in one hand and his forty-five in the other, and panned its beam over the rocky dry wash. A shape moved slightly in the moonlit darkness. He sprinted toward the object. The unnerving howl of the coyote split the darkness. Hurry. Hurry.

Scrambling down the rocky slope, Chase lost his footing, rolled, before righting himself. Sharp rocks cut his fingertips. Undeterred, he hurried deeper into the canyon toward the low moans. The coppery odor of blood hung heavy in the air. A painful breath whooshed from his lungs as he approached the body of his friend and medicine man, Joe Spirit Eyes. Bile rose in his throat. No, not again, not Joe!

Lying beside of Joe's lifeless body was a string of beads. Was this something the killer left behind to forewarn this was his signature?

He pressed two fingers to his friend's neck, a faint heartbeat thrumming erratically under his fingers. Joe moaned and Chase leaned closer. "Ju...Judi." His friend called for his wife, but she had crossed into the spirit world, years ago.

Chase raised his head and peered into the darkness. His pulse quickened and his skin tightened as he realized his friend was dying. He glanced around; the night seemed still. Too still. Too quiet. Who or what watched him? He must use his Apache and Navajo ways to interpret his surroundings.

Ignoring the pounding in his ears, he snatched his weapon from his waist. Was the person who'd hurt Joe still here? He crouched and surveyed the scene, ears alert for any unusual sounds. He prayed the Great Spirit would help Joe Spirit Eyes.

Near another large boulder lay a dark form. Chase hurried to investigate and found another body, but this time, he was too late. He turned the stiff corpse over on its side, and eased his wallet out of his pocket. Under the beam of the flashlight, Chase confirmed the man's ID, with a sad heart. Terry Silver Moon, friend and medicine man, was dead.

Joe moaned again and Chase rushed back to his side, squatting next to him, the odor of blood stronger than before. A pool of blood surrounded Joe's head.

"Joe. Joe, can you hear me?" He removed his lightweight jacket and draped it over his friend's shoulders, hoping the blood loss wouldn't send him into shock.

His friend moved his hand.

"That's right, Joe. Fight. Fight, buddy. I'm going for help. Don't you leave me. Hold on."

Chase scrambled up the rocks, cursing; with few towers near the reservation, his cell phone was useless. He had to reach his car and radio for help. He couldn't let Joe die, not out here in the cold and alone. Not like Terry.

*****

Joe spun from his dreams, trying in vain to cling to their security, but they were as elusive as smoke. Peace wrapped him in a blanket of security but the awful pain yanked him back to the present. Low voices whispered past his ears but he couldn't make out the words. Had the person been talking to him? He wasn't sure. The voice sounded like his friend, Chase, yet he couldn't be sure of that either. Or had Chase's coming to him been part of his dream? So much confusion.

Warm hands touched him. Whose?

Another wave of pain strangled his breath. Please Great Spirit, take this pain.

Joe struggled to open his eyes, but they were so heavy. Nothing in his body seemed to work. His spirit was leaving him. What had happened? How did he end up lying face—down on rocks and dirt? Who had hit him? The recollection wouldn't form.

Many dreams entered his mind, and he welcomed them. Visions of his hot—shot team fighting fires. His wife. Ralan, his son.

Pain snatched him from his dream. Joe breathed through the pain, but it merely enhanced. He drifted into another dream. The warmth of another dream tugged him under—Judi, his lovely wife, smiled and beckoned with her hands. He followed. His heart soared with happiness to be with her again. Visions—varied and often murky—carried him away from the pain and into a land of hopefulness.

＊＊＊＊＊

Chase bolted for his patrol unit. With one hand, he snatched the radio receiver and with the other, he grabbed his thermos of water.

"Dispatch, four-seventeen, I need an ambulance and back up to my location ASAP. Possible homicide scene, one alive." Chase flipped the top on his water and took a long drag; the cold liquid washed the dust from his mouth, but nothing could quench the knot twisting his gut.

The voice on the other end crackled. "Four-seventeen, what's your twenty?"

"Near Old Sand Creek Market, down by the lake." Fear gripped him. "There's a dead man in the wash and one severely injured." Chase's over-zealous voice echoed against the canyon walls.

"Four-seventeen, copy. Back up en route along with EMS." The dispatcher's calm voice echoed back to him.

"Ten-four, please hurry." Chase flung the receiver into the seat, grabbed his first aid kit, his medicine bag, pivoted on his heels and ran back to Joe. The thought of losing Joe, his friend and teacher of the medicine ways, pierced his heart.

Kneeling beside his friend, he opened the first aid kit. He pulled the top from the cleaning solution and rifled through his kit for sterile bandages. Afraid to move him too much, he raised his head and placed the bandage around his head wound. Blood was caked in his hair, and the smell of dried blood, death, was more than he could take.

＊＊＊＊＊

The ambulance siren screamed from the scene with Joe Spirit Eyes in the back, lying near death on the cot, en route to the hospital. Chase's stomach balked as it sped away. His lifelong friend's vitals, according to the medic, weren't good. Feeling the need to stay busy, he retrieved his camera, flares from behind the seat of his squad car, and loaded his backpack to begin his investigation. He climbed down into the wash and lugged his equipment over his shoulders. Jagged rocks lined the way through the tough terrain, but Chase took in no hurry. The time for quick action had passed.

Had Terry and Joe been hurt elsewhere and then transported here? Or had someone forced them to climb down into the dry wash before harming them? Both medicine men.

Chase pondered. *What's happening to our medicine men?* Medicine men spend most of their lives learning and teaching the medicine way. They are unique because the can speak to the spirits. They acquire their special skills in numerous ways. Joe gained his through a vision.

Chase closed his eyes, he also through a vision. Some gained their skills through their father being one, or by objects that they possessed.

He wondered about the reoccurring dreams. *Could there be a message I am not grasping?*

He remembered what Joe told him. *"Once you become a medicine man you will be responsible for our people, their lives, their culture and beliefs, and most importantly you become their healer."*

He snapped back to reality. *Their healer. Oh, how he hoped he could be just as good as Joe.*

Chase lit the flares and positioned them in a large circle around the body. He scanned it for any visible evidence. The camera flashed as he took pictures from various angles, then sketched the scene on a notepad. Then he stepped over to where Joe had lain and set the flares to illuminate that area. Again, he took more photos.

Had Joe merely been at the wrong place at the wrong time? Did he stumble upon something? Or had he been targeted? Chase scratched the back of his neck and glanced back at the corpse. Who could be doing this? He climbed back to the top of the canyon to wait for the Feds to arrive.

He leaned against his dirty truck and folded his arms. Headlights approached, bouncing along the unmaintained road leading to Point of Pines. Even the police station needed work, and most reservation roads lacked funds for upkeep and repairs.

The late— model, black truck pulled next to Chase's patrol unit. He smiled when he recognized the driver, Harmony Wind Dancer, a reporter from the *Apache Signal Newspaper*, who'd covered the murders from the beginning, the second one for the month. Joe's death would make it three. He shuddered at the thought.

Harmony opened the door and stepped out of her truck. Even in the moonlight, her legs looked great in a pair of denim shorts. Chase swallowed desire. She hadn't changed at all, she's more beautiful than ever. *Will I ever get over her?*

Their relationship hadn't worked out, much to his disappointment. He'd heard the rumors spoken about their. His friend Joe had told him many thought the secrets he kept about his life on the Navajo Reservation had caused them to split. Half Apache and half Navajo, he kept many secrets about himself and his people; secrets an inquisitive reporter like Harmony wanted to know because her curiosity didn't stop with her job.

"Hey, Chase."

"We need to stop meeting like this."

Harmony tossed her long hair over her shoulder, the impatient gestured a gentle reminder of their time together. "Right. Murder, mayhem and midnight madness."

He stepped toward to her. "You always were great at alliteration, Ms. Reporter."

She took a step back and reached into her truck for a pad and pencil. "So, what can you tell me about this murder? Heard on the radio coming here that there were two victims?"

"One man dead, Terry Silver Moon, and one severely injured, Joe Spirit Eyes."

Harmony gasped. "No, not Joe? How bad?"

"Head injuries. Major loss of blood. It doesn't look good."

"Any similarities to the other murder?" She glanced around. "Where did it happen?"

Chase jerked his head in the direction of the dry wash. "In the gully, near the rocks and boulders."

She stepped in the direction he'd indicated. Chase's hand snaked out and grabbed her arm. "Where are you off to?"

"I want to get some shots of the crime scene."

"You know better. Your footsteps could compromise the scene. I've got the area cordoned off."

She faced him. "You can't keep me from going down there. I have a right to see. I'm a member of the press."

Chase sighed; the woman could be so headstrong at times. "I'll take you down, but you cannot go beyond the yellow tape. Am I clear?"

"Yes, Mr.-Officer-of-the-Law."

"You drive me crazy, you know that?" He cupped her elbow with his hand.

She tossed him a smile. "Yeah, but you like it."

That was his biggest problem; he liked her too much. "Come along. Watch your step. The climb down is treacherous."

As they made their way down the steep slope, Chase heard pebbles coming toward him so he turned as Harmony landed in his arms.

"Nice catch."

"You feel as nice as you look."

Harmony turned away. "Shouldn't we get going?"

Chase nodded, turned and stepped forward.

They reached the crime scene, and Harmony clicked off several pictures. As he suspected, her desire to get the whole story had her lifting her foot to step across the yellow tape. He grabbed her around the waist and lifted her away from the tape.

"What are you doing?" She squirmed to get free. "Get your hands off me."

He set her down. "Didn't I ask you not to compromise the scene? Don't you want me to catch whoever hurt Joe?"

"Of course I do. You know how I feel about him."

"Then don't compromise the investigation for a few photos. I've already found some clues, and who knows what I'll find in the morning." His gaze swept the area. "If I let you get any closer, you might obliterate a footprint or push a button torn off in a scuffle into the dirt. Clues I need to protect our people."

Harmony exhaled audibly. "I see your point. Okay, I'll be careful." She turned her eyes on him. Eyes he could barely see in the nighttime, but eyes he remembered as being dark and fringed with thick black lashes. "Will you tell me about the clues you've found so far?"

"The killer left a string of beads." He tugged the evidence bag from his pants pocket, shining his flashlight so she could see. "There's also some petroglyphs drawn on that boulder over there. I suspect the assailant used the victim's blood." Chase scraped the rocks, flecks of the dried blood placed into the evidence bag.

She muttered a prayer. Her gaze swept to the boulder he'd indicated and then back to him. "What kind of symbol?"

"The sign for God of Death. In my opinion, the killer is stating he'll keep killing until I stop him."

"You must stop him." Harmony Wind Dancer reached out to touch his arm.

"Or die trying. Yes, I know." He cleared his throat. If he didn't approach her correctly, her impetuous anger would get them both in trouble. "Harmony, please listen to me. I'm worried about our people. I've just shared some information with you that I don't want made public yet. Give me time to gather more information and then I promise you can print whatever you like."

Harmony smiled and nodded, "Okay, Chase, I'll do it because you said please. But you must promise to give me an exclusive."

"Done." He extended his hand, and they shook. His heart quickened and he became a little dizzy. "Let's go back to our vehicles. I'm waiting for the government agent."

"Good, I'll interview him. If he tells me something, I can print it." Harmony hurried up the rocks.

As he made the ascent, Chase thought of the first murder. A hunter and medicine man, slain as he slept under the night sky. His body badly beaten but what had caused the death? Maybe a blow to the head. The family was devastated when news spread about the murder of Wade Silent River. He'd been a good man. From the evidence gathered at the scene, he'd never seen it coming. Blood oozed from the back of his head. Forensics showed death was immediate, yet he'd still been beaten. The string of beads lay by the victim's feet as if sending a message.

The warning was a puzzle for him to solve and until he did, the murders would continue. How would the Apache people handle another murder? Chaos would ensue if Harmony let something slip in the paper. People would think there was a serial killer among them. Maybe there was?

Once they reached the top, Chase turned to Harmony. "The agent and I have some confidential things to discuss. It's best if you aren't here."

"Confidential? Oh, you and your secrets." She poked her finger against his chest. "Don't give me that hard look. You know I say what's on my mind, and secrets are not the best thing to keep between us."

"That's always been our problem. You always think of what you want and never how it affects others."

Harmony sneered, "You have no right to say that to me. We've gone our separate ways because you refuse to open up about your father, and his mysterious death. When I mention it, you change the subject and refuse to discuss it. Your secrets are too hard to deal with." She turned and stalked to her truck. "I'm tired of your secrets."

He grabbed her arm and spun her around, "This is not the time to discuss this."

"It never is."

✶✶✶✶✶

Chase Spirit Walker had her blood boiling with his secretive nature. She turned the key in the ignition. Nothing. Then it grabbed and turned over, a reminder she had to get it checked. The engine light lit up the dash. Something else to add to her "to do" list.

She cracked her window. "I'm going to Joe's house before I go see him at the hospital. I've been staying there, you know."

Chase nodded, and she pulled away.

The drive to Joe's seemed to take forever. As the truck turned down the long driveway, her eyes rested upon the gate sign, "SACRED HORSE RANCH." Tears filled her eyes. What if Joe didn't survive?

The impaired truck made its way to the front of the log home. Harmony turned the key and climbed out. The old red barn stood to her right. Star Dancer, the old horse that once belonged to Joe's wife, whinnied. As she climbed the steps leading to the wraparound porch, her only thoughts were how she could help Chase with the investigation, report the facts, and keep the two separate.

What if another death occurred in or near Coyote Canyon? Harmony cringed at the thought. The deaths would not cease until Chase found the link between the killer and his cause. What bothered her most was the fact that the killer left warnings directed at Joe and Chase. The string of beads meant the killer was out for revenge.

She shivered as she recalled the string of beads in the evidence bag. They matched the late Judi Spirit Eyes' beadwork, like the ones hanging in Joe's home— the last ones Judi made before she died.

Harmony stepped inside the warmth of the house and reached for the phone to call the Apache Tribal Police. Chase needed to know about Joe's beads. If they were a clue, the sooner he knew, the better for the investigation. The entire reservation could fall into disorder once the news of another murder became public knowledge. The previous one had been kept under wraps for the most part.

Harmony leaned against the wall as she spoke to the dispatcher, "I need to speak to Officer Spirit Walker. Could you please have him stop by Joe Spirit Eyes' home ASAP?"

The dispatcher advised he was already en route. Harmony sat down in the chair, staring out the big oval window. The maroon sky was giving way to a peaceful sunrise. She walked to the kitchen counter and picked up Joe's jar of yellow pollen. She turned and stepped onto the porch. She opened the jar and placed the pollen on her head. She sprinkled some onto the porch and offered a prayer to the spirits:

"Creator, please protect the people from the malicious events. Please give Officer Spirit Walker—Chase—guidance to solve this horrible crime. Protect our people. Thank you for providing us with the things we need each day."

Harmony turned full circle and sprinkled the pollen on her head and the ground around her. She sat down on the porch swing and waited for Chase as the first light of day showered its warmth upon the Arizona landscape.

Chapter 2

Harmony waited for Chase to arrive. The morning sky was breathtaking. The many colors of reds, blues, and oranges showered the many sacred directions forming what appeared to be a medicine wheel, floating across the sky. The hoot of the owl echoed across the porch, sending reflections of what was to come. The owl is an omen of bad luck. It meant death was coming... coming soon.

The sound of a car brought Harmony back to reality. Chase pulled into the circular driveway. Even from her position on the porch, she could see his grim expression. Did he think she meant to continue their earlier argument? He stepped out of the vehicle, and stretched his legs. Though she was no longer dating him, she admitted he was a very handsome man.

"Good morning, Harmony," Chase said behind a yawn.

"Had a long night, didn't you? I'm sure investigating a murder takes time to gather all the evidence. Did Agent St. John arrive at the scene?"

"Yep, she was all over it. She believes it's somebody we all know."

"Really? What makes her think that?" Harmony wished she'd stayed at the scene so she'd been privy to the information—if Chase had allowed it.

"From the evidence we gathered tonight, Agent St. John agrees with me that in both murders the killer left the body lying face down with a string of glass beads next to the victim's body. The beads are the four sacred colors: black, blue, yellow, and white. The fact that all the murders are all medicine men is an angle we are investigating. This time he's left another warning. A painting in the victim's blood that means God of Death. If Joe doesn't make it, we're back at square one."

Silence stretched between them. Chase glanced at her, then cleared his throat. Both were silent, obviously ill at ease with each other. "Harmony, I need to talk to you. I have some questions only you can answer."

Harmony stepped off the porch and waved for him to follow her. The beauty of the ranch came full circle as they passed the corral, heading toward a sacred spot that Joe had made for his wife when she needed a place to pray. Joe had shared this spot with her. Jagged rocks protruded out of the side of the canyon. With every step, tiny pebbles scattered to the end of the dry wash.

They emerged at the top of the small hill. Harmony sat on a wooden chair that Joe had made. "Okay, Chase, what troubles you? Speak to me hon."

Chase ran a hand across the back of his neck. "There's no way to say it but straight-out. Joe is a suspect."

"What?"

He silenced her with an outstretched hand. "This isn't easy for me to say, believe me. I've known him for most of my life, we're close friends, and he's my mentor and teaching me the medicine way. I have some unpleasant things I must ask you, things that don't make sense. The beads left at the scene were a trademark of Judi's work. Joe was at the scene of the last murder, too. That, combined with the similarity of the beads, makes him a suspect." Chase paused and turned his gaze to the sunrise. "It just seems so strange because now he is a victim. Maybe he's not working alone and his partner done this to him."

Harmony couldn't believe he truly suspected Joe.

He turned his dark eyes to her and continued. "What about Ralan? Do you see him often? Do you know he blamed Joe for his mother's death?"

Harmony stood and fisted her hands on her hips. "Leave Joe out of this. He would never harm anyone. Ralan has turned his life around and is an important part of our community on the reservation. He's a respected horse trainer, you know this. Hell, Ralan helps me here on the ranch."

Chase turned toward the mountains, obviously lost in thought. Silence screamed between them. Finally, he turned to her. "It shames me to suspect my friend. His son, too. But Agent St. John thinks..."

"Whose word means more to you? Agent St. John's or your longtime friends? What does the Great Spirit tell you?"

Chase stared at his feet. "Joe is my best friend. He means a lot to me." He reached out and trailed a finger down her cheek. "So do you. I hate it when we argue. I hope you forgive me for my cross words."

Harmony faced him, "Yes, I can and do forgive you. Your friendship is important to Joe and to me. We have to stop this bickering and work together. I know it looks strange about the beads. It haunts me, too. I have thought time and again. Hell, I can't even stop thinking of it."

"I'm plagued by dreams, haunting dreams." Chase confessed.

"I have no answers, only more questions. I wanted to speak to you about the beads in Joe's house, but I see you already know."

Harmony turned away as hurtful sobs rushed through her. She wanted to know the truth as much as he did.

Chase wrapped his hand around her arm and motioned for her to head back toward the house. Peace surrounded them. They headed toward the barn where Star Dancer, Judi's horse, belonged. The serene surroundings added to the calmness. Harmony gazed imperceptivity at Chase. Would they—could they— remain friends? When this was over?

Chase stopped abruptly. He stroked his head. Then a vision flashed before his eyes. Joe was innocent. Coyote was at work here. He was tricking the mind to put the focus on Joe.

"Are you okay?"

He stumbled, righted himself. "Yes, a vision of the trickster at work."

"I knew that Joe was being framed."

He placed his hand into hers and nodded toward the pathway.

When they arrived back at the house, Harmony broke the silence. "Chase, you must find the killer. I'll help as much as I can. I will guide you according to my dreams. That's all I can do. I'm almost like a daughter to Joe, so maybe if I stay by his side I can sense something more to tell you."

"Harmony, you are a forgiving woman. Thank you."

Harmony winked, dismissing the intrusion. He took her hand and stepped toward her. She gazed into his eyes.

"Chase, your heart yearns for justice. You must speak the truth to your heart or you will never be free of the past that haunts you. Your spirit must be centered with the Mother Earth to find the killers, to find the justice you need."

Harmony reclaimed her hand and continued into the house, then shut the door behind her.

Chase stood on the porch. The vision was a sign. He smiled for his friend and mentor was innocent. Now to find the killer.

＊＊＊＊＊

The following day, Chase sat in his patrol vehicle outside the gates of the peeling stucco building of the Apache Tribal Police Station.

A tapping on his window brought his attention full circle. Chase turned quickly to find Harmony Wind Dancer and Agent St. John standing at his car door. He rolled down the window.

"What are you thinking so hard about?" Harmony asked.

"There is a killer among us and our people live in fear. Joe Spirit Eyes is lying in the hospital in critical condition, not sure if he will live."

Agent St. John peered into his window. "Did you visit Joe Spirit Eyes?"

He glared at the persistent agent. She'd already tried and convicted Joe in her mind. "Yes, this morning. He could barely talk. I know him too well to believe he'd break the law. Leave him alone."

Harmony nodded. "Joe is a good man. He's letting me stay at his house until my home is ready."

Chase opened his door and stood, grinning at Harmony, "Well, we finally agree on something."

Harmony walked beside him and held the door as they each filed into the police station. Voices echoing up and down the hallway seized their attention.

Agent St. John turned to face Chase. "I have a conference with my superior on this case and then I'm going to call it a day. Call me if anything develops."

He nodded and headed toward his office. The dark, dusky hallway held little light, but Harmony's footsteps echoed behind him. Key in hand, he stopped to unlock his office door. The lock jammed. A snapping sound turned Chase toward Harmony as the heel broke and she fell into Chase's arms, breaking her fall. "Are you okay?" He pulled her into a hug. She felt so good in his arms.

"Chase, we're friends, nothing more."

He released her and walked into the foul-smelling office. His disorderly desk sat by a window. Chase opened it, hoping fresh air would dilute the odor. He sat on the corner of his desk, staring at the ever-growing pile of paperwork.

"Do you want to talk about it?" Harmony asked.

"About what? That you only want to be friends, or about the murders?"

Harmony crossed her arms and glared.

Chase shrugged. "I'm troubled over these murders. I hate that I questioned Joe's honesty. What do you think, Harmony? Do you think Joe or his son Ralan could be involved?"

Harmony fumbled with a pen. "We've already discussed this. You know I feel that there is no way that Joe is involved, Ralan I can't say. Yet I know you have to follow every lead and piece of evidence. Go with your instincts, and I believe you will find the truth."

Chase reached and smoothed her hair "Thank you."

"Why are you struggling with Joe and Ralan's innocence? I have something to tell you. I had a dream last night. It was like I could see with the killer's eyes. He had a scar on the back of his left hand."

"That's interesting. That would explain the other blood type we found at the scene."

Harmony glared. "You never mentioned there were two types of blood found. "Chase leaned back in his chair, folded his arms behind his head and he placed his boots up on his desk. "I can't reveal all my evidence. I keep thinking about when Judi had the accident. There were a lot of threats made by Ralan and other kinfolk. Ralan took his mother's death hard."

Harmony sat on a chair in front of his desk. "Yeah, I remember that, but it was nobody's fault."

"Don't you recall the threats made on Joe's life? Judi was having dizzy spells and yet Joe still took her out on that ride. Why did he do that? Now, there are murders occurring on the reservation and at each crime scene we find the string of glass beads that match Judi's. Add to that, Joe is often at the scene. Evidence is mounting and I can't ignore it. I don't know what to think."

"I see where you're going, but there's no evidence at the scene actually tying him to the murder. And he's been hurt too."

Chase set up and put a few files into his briefcase. "It's been a long day, and I've had little sleep since all this started. I'm going home to rest." He stood and came around the desk. "I heard the owl hoot and I fear another murder will occur."

Standing on her missing heel, Harmony stumbled into Chase. His arm wrapped around her.

Their eyes locked. Chase pushed her long, black hair from her shoulder, moments from confessing his love for her still. He lowered his head, breathed a kiss to her neck, and felt a sense of satisfaction when he felt her shiver.

"I should go. It's getting late, and I have a lot of things to do."

Chase followed her out of his office and down the hallway. She limped as she walked. "You remind me of a bird with a broken wing."

She slapped his arm.

He chuckled, and reached to open the door. The chill of the night rushed in.

Harmony shivered. "Tonight's going to be chilly. Most of the nights are warm here, but tonight Mr. Chill is creeping in."

Chase gently placed his tribal jacket around her shoulders. "Wear my jacket home. Have a good night."

She stopped and gazed up at him.

"Chase, would you like to go get a cup of coffee before we call it a day?"

"That would be nice." Any time he spent with her soothed his soul.

He opened the door to his patrol unit, watching her every move. She smiled at him when she climbed into her truck. As he pulled out of the parking lot behind her, Chase hoped that they could work things out. The back lights on her truck were out, but as he followed her down Indian Route Road he remained lost in his own thoughts of her.

They pulled into the parking lot of Red's Diner. He pulled up beside her vehicle.

"I may have to give you a ticket."

"For what?"

"You have no tail lights."

Harmony chuckled. "I meant to get them fixed but with what's been going on, I forgot."

He wrapped his arm around her neck. The ding of the door as they walked in startled Harmony.

"Lets it here."

As they waited to be served, their eyes locked on one another. Both wanting to say the same thing...*I love you...*

Just as the moment was about to explode, the waitress interrupted their thoughts.

"May I take your order?"

"Just coffee for me, what would you like Harmony?"

"Same for me."

Chase glanced at her. "Do you remember the time we went to get something to eat and we neither one had any money?"

Harmony chuckled. "Oh yes, that was so funny."

The waitress set their coffee down. "Will there be anything else?"

Chase glanced up. "Yes, two BLT's."

The waitress nodded and turned away.

As they waited on their food, silence erupted between them. Feelings of how they each felt for one another floated among them.

"Here is your BLT's."

As they were eating, Chase's radio went off.

"There has been a car accident. Guess I should take this since I am closer."

"Okay, it's getting late and I am getting tired. See you tomorrow?"

"Of course, I will miss you until then."

Harmony smiled and winked as he headed out the glass door.

Chase headed to his patrol unit as the dreadful reminder of the murders crept back into his mind. Would another innocent person die tonight by the hands of a mad man who thought his cause was real and his purpose sustained? Would serenity and safety return to the reservation?

Chapter 3

Harmony jolted awake from a deep, troubling dream. In her twenty-nine years of life on mother earth she had never dreamed so much as she had since the beginning of the murders. She sat up and cast her eyes toward the window. The moon hung high in the sky, casting shadows on the unrelenting restlessness. She felt the presence of uneasiness in the area. She eased out of the creaky wooden bed and stared out the window into the darkness of the night.

The presence of Joe Spirit Eyes loomed inside his home. Harmony felt his presence, the coldness, the anger. The screeching of the owl confirmed what Joe had taught her in the short while since she had returned to the reservation after obtaining her journalism degree from Arizona College in Tucson.

"*Ba'ts'ose*, Coyote tells me in his own words what has happened," Harmony whispered softly, a circle of fog formed on the window. "*Da'itsaahi*, death has arrived once again in Coyote Canyon."

Kaboom!!! Lightning sent rays of light crisscrossing through the night sky. The smell of rain was in the air, mixed with the scent of death.

Harmony walked down the dark hallway, taking each step hesitantly. The sky was alive from the storm brewing. She walked into the kitchen, turned on the coffeepot, and stared at the clock.

"Four-fifteen, time of death." She wrote it down on the pad of paper that lay by the phone.

A sudden beep caused her to turn quickly. It was the signal the coffee was done, and the aroma made her stomach rumble. She smiled and reached into the cabinet and removed her favorite mug that Joe had given her when she'd returned to the rez, to celebrate her landing a job as head reporter for her people. She eased the cabinet door shut when suddenly when she saw a reflection of somebody outside. She eased around to find nothing there. She glanced down at the mug ...*A hawk and an eagle hung from the inner circle of a dream catcher.*

The legend of the dream catcher was a centuries— old tradition. Harmony eased backward against the log walls and thought of her father's tale of the legend. *Dreams are special, given to us from the spirits of our ancestors. The hole in the middle of the web allows all of our good dreams to pass through but the bad dreams are captured and not allowed to pass, and when the morning sun rises, the bad dreams are burned away. The dream catcher blesses the sleeper with good luck and harmony.*

Thunder shook the earth. Harmony was startled from her comforting memories. As she poured her coffee, a strange, rattling noise echoed from the front porch. Setting her mug down, she walked over to the window, pulled the curtains back, and peeked outside into the pouring rain. Nothing but darkness.

She turned and walked to the table, where Joe kept a gun. She picked it up and headed toward the front door leading to the porch. Walking slowly, trying to take in her surroundings, she noticed nothing strange.

As she neared the porch swing, her heart pounded in her ears, her hands began to sweat. Lying in the swing was a string of beads. As the storm grew more intense, a vivid flash of light streaked across the porch. She raised the gun to protect herself from the evil that surrounded her.

Harmony whispered, "The *its'izilheehi*, the murderer, was here. Her heart beat rapidly as her shaking hands tightened on the gun. "The killer walked on this porch. Watching me." A shudder of foreboding swept through her. "I have to contact... must contact Chase."

She stepped back into the house, her hands shaking like Jell-O. How could the killer get so close to her without her sensing it? Her special abilities should have warned her. What happened?

✶ ✶ ✶ ✶ ✶

She reached for her cell phone and dialed Chase. *Of course it goes to his voice mail.*

"Chase, its Harmony, Some weird things are going on here. I believe the murderer was on my porch. Please call as soon as you get this message.

She pushed the hang-up button on the phone. "Well I guess I should call the office to, maybe he is in a meeting.

"Officer Spirit Walker, please." Harmony fought to keep her fear at bay.

"I'm sorry, but Officer Spirit Walker has not yet arrived for his shift."

"This is Harmony Wind Dancer, and it's very important that he calls me back ASAP."

The dispatcher sensed the urgency in her voice. "Ms. Wind Dancer, I'm going to call him at home right now."

"Thank you. I'll be waiting."

Harmony sat down in Joe's favorite recliner, and rubbed her eyes. "Why was the killer here? Was he after me?"

Lost in thought, when the phone rang, she jumped. "Hello, this is Harmony."

Chase's voice echoed through the phone, and relief filled her. She could breathe again.

"Good morning, Harmony. What are you doing up so early?"

Harmony's voice cracked as she spoke, "Chase, you need to come over here as soon as you can. The killer was here! He left a string of beads on the porch swing. I know he was watching me through the window."

"Harmony, are you okay? Are you sure he's gone? Stay inside and don't touch the beads. I'm just a few miles away. I'll be there soon."

Harmony sat in a daze. "Okay, Chase, I just don't understand why he was here. What's going on?"

"Keep the doors locked and don't open them for anybody. It will be okay. Do you hear me?"

"Yes, Chase I hear you. Please hurry."

After she hung up, and his voice died, she realized the pain of losing his love still haunted her. She would not let this terror scare her into admitting she loved him. He would just walk away as he'd done before. She couldn't, and wouldn't, allow him to leave her again.

The morning sun cascaded her face over Mother Earth. Even though Chase instructed her to stay inside, Harmony stepped out onto the porch. She could not let the sun come up without her presence. She sat on the steps, with a jar of corn pollen in her hand, taking in the beautiful views of her homeland. It was a custom to offer the corn pollen every morning as a blessing for the people, and nothing was going to keep her from doing it. She faced the east and sprinkled the pollen on the ground, turned to the right and dusted the ground again. She repeated the steps twice more, turning in the four sacred directions, and then sprinkled the pollen on her head. She opened her eyes and whispered, *"dolelgo at'ee, amen."*

The barrel cactus displayed its unique beauty against the desert scenery. It had grown over the years, standing at least five feet tall. She recalled how Joe had told her how his wife, Judi, admired the cactus during the summer months. The flowers that sprouted on it ranged from orange, yellow, to red. The top of the cactus where the blooms would flourish was breathtaking.

She turned her head toward the sacred mountain in the distance where all the gods and ancestors lived. Connecting with the elements of Mother Earth helped the surging ache in her heart. The murders, Joe's injuries, and Chase? She shook the last thought from her mind, and gazed back at the horizon.

Then the image of the Mount Graham Sacred Run entered her mind. This was very important to her people. It usually began in the month of *Binii' Idichihe*, July, or month of Face Turns Red. Although its starting point varied each year, it would be at the Point of Pines, which is in the Northern part of the reservation. Harmony decided she was going to run this year. She had missed so many. She closed her eyes and envisioned the beauty of Point of Pines. The massive meadows, the luxuriant green grass that covered the land, the shading of the evergreen pine that provided protection and the abundance of wildlife scurrying around brought the connection of the early morning blessings.

Over the many years, the run had grown important to Chase.

Now, she was learning why. It served a purpose to our runners. It answered many blessings for their people. It taught their young the importance of the Apache sacred mountain, but most importantly, it renewed the tribe's spiritual beliefs. Another sacred site, Old San Carlos Monument, came to mind, along with its spiritual importance to the Apache. This was where many of their ancestors died, the place where Geronimo walked, and where many bodies were buried under the water.

Harmony jolted back to the present from the incoming noise of tires crunching on gravel as it sped up the driveway. The crisp, cool morning sent a chill up her spine. Harmony squinted as the sun rose higher into the sky, blessing a new day.

She stood to welcome Chase, relieved she was no longer alone.

"Good morning, Chase." Harmony swallowed hard.

Chase bounded from his vehicle, his anger and concern evident, *"Doo idits'ada da*, you do not listen! What are you doing outside? I told you to stay in and not open the door for any one."

Harmony raised an eyebrow, *"Dahbiida*, morning to you too."

"Don't ignore me. You could have been hurt." Chase's face was grim.

"Calm down. I know it was *begodzidi*, dangerous, but the morning sun was blessing Mother Earth and I too, had to offer my blessing. Besides, the attacker would not stand on this porch with the sun in his face."

Chase ignored her. "Show me the beads."

She turned toward the swing and motioned.

Chase stepped to the swing and examined them. "Yes, the killer's been here. The beads match the others left at the scene." He glanced around, obviously observing the area. "What's this?" He pointed to the image of the owl smeared onto the siding of the home just below the kitchen windowsill. It appeared to be drawn in blood.

"Harmony, did you notice this?"

Harmony gasped, and jumped backwards with sweat beading on her face. "It's an omen of death!"

He reached for her hand. "It's okay. I would never let anything happen to you."

Chase's cell phone rang and he walked away, speaking to his dispatcher. Harmony realized by the sad expression on his face, the call was bringing more bad news.

"Okay, Harmony, I want you to gather some things and go to my house. I'm certain you're in danger. Promise me you'll stay there and keep the doors locked. Meanwhile, I have to go. There's been another body found about four miles from here. I'll return as soon as the scene is secured."

"Chase, what's going on? The killer is after me, isn't he? He wants to haunt and scare me. Well, it's not going to work." She startled herself with the defiance in her tone.

Chase placed his arm around her shoulder and kissed her hair. "We'll catch the person responsible. It's just a matter of time. I promise I won't let anything happen to you."

Harmony managed to smile but in her heart, she realized there would be more killings, a lot more. She wondered if she would end up being one of them.

*****

Chase's heart pounded in his chest. Who was the next one? He prayed the chaos would end soon. The dirt road lead him to a horrific scene. He climbed out of his patrol unit.

"Hey Chase. The victim is Harold White Horse. He was hit from behind."

"Noooo. He was going to help with the annual giving program. He is ninty-seven years old. What kind of damn threat is that? Whoever is killing off our medicine men are depleting our people of our medicine way. "

Chase walked over to the ravine and stood over Harold. He blessed him in the traditional Apache way. His heart was heavy. This man had a lot to offer to his people. He turned slightly and noticed something wrote on a huge boulder.

He walked closer and written in blood the words...SHE IS NEXT...

Fear and anger crept through his veins. The beaded sweat from the desert sun radiated on his skin. He knew the threat was for him directly.

He snapped a picture of the scene, including the threat and headed back to his patrol unit. His mind and heart was torn for his people, especially the only woman he had ever loved. He had to protect her at all cost.

The drive home gave him a chance to think through some of today's events. The killer wanted to taut him. He was doing a damn good job at it. The face of Harmony filled his thoughts. He loved her so much. He would protect her with his own life. He couldn't wait to see her.

*****

Harmony gathered a suitcase and headed to Chase's house. He proved his love for her this morning as he demanded her to move to his house. She had always loved him.

"Now, our love has a true chance. He will open up to me soon. I will be his woman and mother to his children."

The thoughts brought a smile to her face. She stepped off the porch and headed to her truck. She cranked it and it stalled.

"Damn it. I have to get this thing fixed."

Another hard turn of the ignition, and it cranked. She pulled out of Joe's driveway, looking back at the house. Why was all of this happening to her people? Her trust and faith would remain with Chase and the Creator. They would win.

Chapter 4

In a daze, Harmony drove to Phoenix to check on Joe in the hospital, to which he'd been airlifted. The scenery changed from mountaintops to cacti. The towering cacti were breathtaking. They stood proudly around her, revealing their inner sanctity.

Harmony prepared for the stop at the Oak Flats Sacred Site. This was the place her people came to ask the spirits for help. Many spirits lived here. She needed them to keep her safe and return her to the homeland of their people.

She turned into the dry, graveled area. The previous rain had not helped with the drought. She eased her vehicle into the spot where Joe had taken her when she had lost her parents. Once she turned off the engine and stepped out of her vehicle, the spirits made their presence known. She removed the jar of corn pollen from her backpack. Pollen held many uses; but usually it was used for blessings, for protection, understanding, and forgiveness. She sprinkled her head and the ground in front of her, the traditional way of offering prayers for protection during travels.

"Creator, please bless our people. I offer these prayers to the *biyideel*, spirits, which walked on this sacred land. *Da'itsaahi*, death has arrived on our reservation. We need many blessings. Our faith holds true. Thank you for providing our people with all their needs. *Doleelgo at'ee*, Amen."

Again, Harmony sprinkled pollen onto the earth and herself, coming full circle. She opened the door to her vehicle, but her eye caught the movement of the creatures of this sacred land; *tsegadag histas*, scorpion and *a tl iish*, snake, slithered from the space they called home. These very dangerous creatures reminded her of the killer that stalked and killed on the reservation, and she shuddered.

She put the vehicle in reverse and backed out of the area, not taking her eyes off the creatures. Her journey had just begun. Joe had told her the path you chose decided which journey you would walk. So this must be her path. Harmony tried to stay positive about Joe's condition and not give into her fears. The doctors had said he would be lucky to pull through. The blow to the head had caused massive hemorrhaging inside the brain. Harmony tried to keep a grasp on hope.

Her mind shifted to the mining company, trying to take the sacred site. The steel mineshaft stood erect. It was an eyesore to the area. Her heart wept in silence. *How could they just come onto our land and desecrate it like this?*

She drove on in silence, her mind thinking of the consequences of such actions, taking note of the beautiful red rock formations. Then the traffic started to get hectic.

Rush hour traffic on the 101 was heavy. As she turned into the hospital parking lot she took note of Ralan, Joe's son, sitting in his car. She pulled in beside him. She waved in his direction when she climbed out of her truck, but he seemed lost in his thoughts and did not return her greeting.

She walked closer to his car. The passenger window was open. "Hello, Ralan. How are you? I'm so sorry about your father. He's a good man."

Ralan's angry expression startled her. "I don't need to hear how sorry you are. That man in there is the reason my mother died. I don't even know why I'm here."

Harmony exhaled a shocked gasp. "Ralan, your mother loved him and would not want you to blame him for her death."

Ralan grabbed Harmony by the wrist. "Don't speak of my mother. Do you understand me?" His eyes squinted with anger. His jaw clenched with emotion.

Pain radiated to her elbow. "Let go! Ralan, you're hurting me!"

Anger flashed in his eyes. He released his grip, pushing her backward. Harmony stared at him as he backed his sports car out of the parking lot. Tires squealed.

She rubbed her wrists as she walked into the hospital, willing herself not to be afraid. Ralan was beyond angry. She had to tell Chase. She stepped onto the elevator, and depressed the button for the eighth floor, ICU. As the doors opened, a familiar face turned toward her. It was Joe's brother, Ray.

"Hello, Ray, how's Joe doing?" Harmony asked.

Ray's face revealed the sadness. "Well, the doctor says each passing day he remains with us is a good sign. We're unsure if there will be brain damage until he wakes. Ralan has not been to see him and the family is getting very upset at his disrespect."

Harmony was shocked. *Then why was Ralan in the parking lot?*

Perhaps she could soften things for Ray. "I'm sure everything will work out. Ralan is going through a hard time. He lost his mother, and now his father's life is uncertain."

Ray nodded. "I hope so. Thank you for coming, Harmony. I'll be in the cafeteria if you need me."

Harmony hugged him. "He's like a father to me."

She walked down the sterile hallway to the ICU waiting room, feeling a sense of pity for Ralan. He had lost so much. The wait to see Joe would be nerve racking. All the sadness on the faces of the people waiting to see their loved one's but knowing at any moment they could be gone. Like Joe; the thought terrified her.

She sat down in the vinyl seat and flipped through Country Cottage Magazine. Then the people started gathering at the door, waiting to go see their loved ones. Seconds later a dark haired male nurse opened the door. They filed through. As she made her way to Joe's room, her face felt hot. She got to the door and stopped.

"Please give me the strength to see him."

Harmony pushed the door and stepped inside. She grabbed her stomach. She stepped around the curtain. She gasped, nearly choking. The IV's and all the machines hooked up to him. Is this the only reason he is alive? She leaned against the wall and sobbed.

"Creator, please help Joe. He's a good man and he loves his people. Heal him."

She walked over to his bedside and placed a kiss on his head.

"I love you Joe. Beat this for me."

She stood and stared at him. Her heart broke as she thought of how he had helped her through so many things. He had to make it.

She turned and left, with her heart in her hand.

＊＊＊＊＊

Harmony sat in her truck, pounding the steering wheel. "Why is this happening? How many more are there going to be?"

She turned the key and drove out onto the freeway. The trip back home would be hard. She pushed the gas pedal and turned up the radio. She drove in silence until her favorite country singer came over the speakers. *Luke Bryan's song Kick the Dust Up."*

She reached for the knob and turned the music loud as she headed back to the reservation. For a little while *Luke* took her mind off the problems in life.

She drove and took in the views of the protruding red rocks. Oak Flats would be coming up soon and she would do her usually stop and offer a prayer.

Oak Flat came into view, she flipped on her blinker and pulled into the sacred site. She pulled and pushed the truck into park. She stepped out.

"Creator and our ancestors, please protect our people, especially Joe. Give Chase the direction he needs to travel to stop this. Our people need you. Thank you."

She jumped back in the truck and headed toward the precious mountains she called home. The only man she would ever love would be waiting for her. A smile plastered across her face. *"Yes, I love you Chase."*

* * * * *

The dispatcher echoed over the radio a fire was burning in the area. Chase followed the smell of smoke down the dirt road. His nose burned. His fears grew with the turn of the winding road. Did the killer have a new tactic? A fire would get their attention, quickly.

As he rounded the next curve, smoke enveloped the patrol unit. Chase coughed and struggled to roll up his window. He slammed on the brakes when the heavy soot obscured his vision; even so, his vehicle went into the ditch, hitting the mountainside. The patrol car flipped. His head smacked the window. His vision blurred and something warm trickled into his eye. He fumbled for the radio to inform the dispatcher of his accident. Before he could sign off, everything went black.

When Chase came to, he found himself slumped over the steering wheel, his patrol unit sideswiped against the mountain. He rubbed his head and tried to focus on where he was. The acrid smell of smoke was everywhere. He managed to climb out and stand as another unit arrived on the scene.

"Chase, are you all right?" his fellow officer asked.

"Yeah, man, I think so. I don't know what happened other than I rounded the curve and the smoke filled my unit and I hit the ditch, flipping and landed against the mountain side."

Chase walked with his friend's assistance. They waited for the ambulance to arrive. "Take me to the edge of the dry wash. Is this another warning from the killer?"

Peering through the smoke, Chase scanned the area. Uneasiness washed over him. There!

"Look! Something's moving. We have to get down there to help."

"You're hurt. Your head is bleeding. I'll go."

A wave of nausea swept over him. Chase slumped down and nodded.

Chase lay on the ground wondering if this would be another crime scene, and what would be found this time. Where was his fellow officer? Pushing with his hands, he stretched and stared into the ravine at nothing but smoke.

"Greg! Do you see anything? Are you okay?"

Silence enveloped the area. Adrenaline rushed through his body. Chase stood, and walked toward the edge of the canyon, placing his boot sideways as he scaled the rocky surface. He had to help his friend. His vision blurred. His head spun. Before Chase could steady himself he fell and slid to the bottom of the canyon, and his body came to rest against another body. Another medicine man. Craig Many Moons. And obviously lifeless. Then his world went black again.

Images of his life floated in front of him. He wondered if he would see Harmony again. Everything was peaceful but moving in a frantic mode. Chase wondered if he was now in the spirit world and if so, would he see his father? He had so many questions for him. Why did he have to die before he got to know him? What happened on the Navajo Reservation? The mystery of shape shifting, could he do it? Did he have a twin who'd died at birth? His mother had explained to him that his father was trying to uncover a ring of artifact smugglers when he'd been found murdered in a canyon.

He tugged against the darkness pulling at him and eased into a helpless deep sleep.

$$\star\,\star\,\star\,\star\,\star$$

Upon waking, he found himself on a cot with EMS personnel hovering over him. Chase felt a sudden, sharp pain in the back of his head.

"*Kaa ansht'ee* I'm hurt. Where am I?"

"Sir, you're going to be all right. You've suffered a blow to the head. Lie still."

Movement only caused more dizziness. He slumped backward onto the cot and lost consciousness, the vision came as he was passed out. He's driving down the road, to his home. Chase was en route to gather his *diyinihii,* his sacred things to pray. Dirt turned to pavement. At the stop sign, he glanced up at the sky. A red tailed hawk flew over his truck and into his path.

Chase could not take his eyes off the fascinating bird of prey. He whispered, "*Deelicho*, hawk, what's the warning you are trying to deliver to me?"

The hawk's cry pierced like a knife, echoing through Chase's head. The bird of prey was delivering a warning from the ancestors who lived before him, walking the good red road. The vision drew Chase from his truck. The hawk soared, his chocolate- brown coloring and white breast stark against the sky, and its red tail fluttered in the sun. It swooped, crossing Chase's path, and then perched on a nearby fence post.

It was as if Chase were talking in a barrel. "My friend, what warning do you have for me? My grandfather told me many years ago about the sharp eye and brave heart of the hawk and how it soars close to Grandfather Sun."

34

Light flickered. Dimensions clashed. The hawk transformed into an elder of famous mention. Geronimo stared into Chase's eyes. "The killer is among our people and you are the only one who can stop him. You know him but you cannot see that he is the one, because he's the least likely. You are of the medicine way. You have the power as I do to be a shapeshifter. You will solve this soon." Then the hawk flew off in the direction of Grandfather Sun.

Chase was in awe. He yawned, whispering, "Someone is missing me." To the Apache, yawning means that someone misses you. Then in a flash, Chase was awake, aware that he was moaning as the ambulance lurched forward.

"Wait, wait, I have to help with the scene!" He pulled at the medic's sleeve. "Where is Greg? He needs my help."

"No, you've been badly injured. You need to go to the hospital." The medic tied his arms down and continued to work on an IV.

Chase continued to slip in and out of consciousness. He had to return to the scene. Another family would grieve for a loved one. But why was Craig Many Moons on the Apache Reservation? He lived on the Navajo Reservation.

The hawk!!! *Goyaale*, Geronimo, his ancestor of Chiricahua descent, had come to him in a vision. *Him? A shapeshifter? Was this all a dream, or was the vision real?* Drugs coursed through the IV and darkness consumed him.

Chapter 5

Chase squirmed. He had to get off the cot. The elderly nurse came back into the room as he rose on an elbow.

"You better lie back down. You have a concussion. The doctor will be in to see you soon."

The elder was wise and he should listen or he would regret it. He tried to focus around the room and not so much on the murders. The door swung open and Harmony rushed in.

"Chase, are you okay?" She hurried to his side, concern on her beautiful face. "I couldn't believe it when I heard you'd been brought here." Her cool hand rested on his cheek.

Chase smiled. He liked nothing better than her fussing over him. "Yeah, I'll be okay. The doctor says I have a concussion, but I'll be fine."

"Lie back and rest. I know you better than anyone. You're trying to figure out a way to get out of here so you can return to your job. I'm not leaving and neither are you, until the doctor says so."

The stubborn tone in her voice drove Chase crazy. He loved her and now he knew she loved him. He cupped his hand to the back of her head, and pulled her close and kissed her.

The doctor walked in, interrupting their kiss and conversation. "Okay, young man, I know you want to leave, but you're going to have to wait until morning. I'm keeping you overnight for observation."

"Doc, I'm fine. I've got a murder to solve," Chase protested.

"It's okay, Dr. Overstreet. I'll make sure he spends the night. Will he have a room soon?" Harmony gave Chase a warning look. He cocked an eyebrow at the outward exchange, enjoying her take-charge attitude.

"Yes, he's assigned to room three thirty –four."

Chase listened to the two deciding his fate. Although his head hurt too much to laugh, his heart was light when he chimed in, "Listen, I'm the patient here. Looks as though between the two of you, I have no choice but to stay. Although I disagree, I'll spend one night. I expect to be discharged by seven in the morning."

"We'll see, Chase. See you at seven." The doctor walked out.

Chase stared at Harmony. He would have done the same if it had been her. The nurse returned, breaking the silence.

"You have to rest so I'm giving you a sedative to help you sleep."

"Okay, goes in my arm," Chase instructed.

The nurse chuckled. "I'm afraid I need a little more meat. It has to go into your bottom. Yours isn't special, son. I've seen plenty."

Chase could feel the heat of a blush on his face as he turned to his side. The nurse pulled the sheet down, exposing his butt.

Harmony tittered. As he drifted into a deep sleep, her laughter echoed in his mind, reminding him just how much he missed her when she wasn't around. He had to remedy that.

*****

The morning sun sparkled through the window, as he woke from a deep sleep. As he gazed around the room, he noticed Harmony lying peacefully sleeping.

"Where's Dr. Overstreet? He said I could leave this morning."

Chase twisted in his bed. His nerves were getting the best of him.

"Look, Chase," Harmony consoled. "you have to lie still as Dr. Overstreet, walked in."

"Okay, young man, I have your discharge papers, but you have to take it easy."

"Okay doc, got it. Where do I sign?"

Chase scribbled his name on the papers and jumped off the bed to dress. His mind was groggy from the medication but he had to get out of there.

"Harmony, he needs to take it slow for several days. Do what you can to make sure of that."

"Yes, Dr. Overstreet I'll be right by his side and do the best I can."

Chase came out of the bathroom, smiled, and put on his boots.

38

"Let's go, Harmony. I have a lot to do today."

They rolled Chase into the elevators. Harmony turned to him. "Remember what the doctor said, you must take it easy." Chase nodded and kept his eye on the elevator doors. As they opened, he jumped out of the wheel chair.

"Come on, Harmony, we have to get to the murder scene."

Harmony's face flushed red. "Chase, I promised the doctor to watch out for you."

"Yeah, I know, but I'm okay."

"Well, let's slow down."

They climbed into the car and Chase revved up the engine. His mind was in fast mode. The scene...the scene.

The tires squealed as Chase pulled out of the hospital entrance.

"We must get there before something disrupts the scene. Maybe I can find a clue everybody else missed."

"Chase, please listen to me. I want you to promise me that you will take it easy."

He glanced at her, smiling.

"Your beautiful and you care."

"Chase, stop it. You will do as I say."

"Yes, Miss boss."

She smiled as they drove down Hwy 60. Mother Earth gave such beautiful scenery. They past Gold Canyon, nestled near Superstition Mountains. They drove in silence until the towering mountains brought them closer to Oak Flat.

"Let's say a prayer to the spirits of Oak Flat."

They pulled in and stood beside each other.

"Great Spirit, we are requesting for your assistance and guide on this situation. We need every ancestor and spirit guide to lead us to redemption. Our people are in dire need. Please help us stop the murders plaguing our reservation."

They turned in the four sacred directions. They faced each other.

"I love you Harmony."

She blushed. "I love you, too."

They climbed back into the truck and headed to their homeland. The drive gave Chase the chance to think about his life and where he wanted to take it from this point. He would become a great medicine man and a husband to Harmony. A father...yes, that would be his dream. First, he had to rid the reservation of the evil and then he would be free.

✶✶✶✶✶

Chase sidestepped down the rock alongside the canyon, where the body of a middle– aged man had been recovered the day before. A canyon wren danced around the area claiming it as his own. Chase smiled as he watched it stand her ground.

He made his way to where the body had been recovered; he stopped abruptly and looked toward the top of the rim. Harmony watched his every move, just as she'd promised the doctor.

"Chase, you're going too fast. Listen to me, or I'll take you home. I only agreed to bring you here because you promised not to overdo it."

"I know. I'm sorry. I just need to make sure procedure was followed."

He combed the area, hoping to find more clues. Chase was about to give up when the unexpected occurred. The wind blew swiftly and caused a tumbleweed to spiral around the area. The movement caught his attention. That's when he saw them. About thirty feet from where he was standing there were petroglyphs drawn on the canyon walls with the victim's blood.

Walking closer, he yelled at Harmony, "Get down here with your camera. I've found something."

"I'll be right there."

Harmony stood her distance until Chase confirmed it was okay to enter the area.

"So, the killer has left us more evidence, huh?"

Chase leaned up against the rocks, "Yeah, the killer is in the clan of the snake and coyote'. He'd confirmed this by the drawing of the animals on these walls. In between, the two animals the sign of death was sketched, a box colored with dark blood and lines in the form of the mountains.

Harmony snapped the pictures. "Chase, what do the mountains represent?"

"The killer is trying to say death reigns in these mountains and will continue until I stop it."

Chase quickly stepped backward, almost falling down the deep canyon. "The *buh*, owl. This is a bad sign. The killer is using witchcraft against our people yet the owl's stet warnings are a deceiver, who tricks us into believing what isn't real. We've got to rethink this murder scene." He slowly glanced around, taking in everything he saw. "We're missing something."

Harmony stared at him, "Chase, do our people really fear the owl?"

Chase's face revealed complete shock, "Harmony, you've been away for a while. You must have forgotten what your parents taught you about the deception of the owl."

Chase turned away from her, hoping she hadn't lost more connections to the beliefs of their people.

So many mysteries... He stared blankly at the entire scene, taking note when a raven flew overhead.

"Harmony, look! A raven soaring across the sky."

The glare from the sun made the enormous bird look magical for he was the bearer of magic.

Chase realized it was time for him to look deeper into his own soul. A time for a vision quest in the sweat lodge or at Oak Flats. Both places served as a spiritual guide.

Chase turned to Harmony. "We must go. The raven has brought a warning to me. There's dark magic here, and the only way to stop it is to have my body cleansed."

Harmony stared at him. "I know how our people feel about the dark magic the raven brings. Joe always said such magic is deceptive. The black raven is known as the void, or the great mystery."

"Yes, you remember your teaching from Joe." Chase motioned it was time to go. He headed back up the steep canyon wall with Harmony on his heels. He was learning the medicine way from his Apache Elders, the medicine men. The raven indicated magic was being used, and Joe would be able to tell him more if he would just wake up, but he'd been in a coma for days. Joe was linked to the murders, but the question was, how?

Reaching the top of the canyon, Chase picked up his mic from the dashboard. "Dispatch, I need to speak to a medicine man right away. Could you please find Lloyd Many Tears? He's one of the best. "

"Ten-four. In reference to?" The lone dispatcher unclicked the mic.

Chase shrugged, "It's in reference to the murders. I need his assistance."

"Ten-four, I'll attempt to call him now."

Climbing into his police unit, he winked at Harmony beside him. His smile was fake, for he was concerned for her welfare. He didn't want her to know how he worried about her. The murderer was seeking revenge, and he feared Harmony might be a target.

"So, do you think Lloyd Many Tears can help you?"

"Yes, I do." He ran his hand over her long dark hair. Then he remembered the eeriness of the deep canyons that resembled the fear he held in his heart for the safety of the only woman he would ever love.

"I'm taking you to my place, where I want you to remain until the killer's caught."

"Okay, although I would be fine at Joe's. Ralan is often there. He sleeps in the barn sometimes." She paused. " I didn't tell you that he frightened me the other day."

"Go on." Chase's brow furrowed.

"I saw him when I went to the hospital, in Phoenix. He was sitting in his car, staring at the building. I walked up and said hello and how sorry I was about his dad, and he grabbed my arm. There's a bruise on my wrist." She pulled the sleeve up.

"Why didn't you tell me about this? How dare he? I'm going to have a long talk with him soon. You're staying at my house. End of discussion." The anger emerged on his face as well as in his voice.

Silence enveloped the unit until the dispatcher's voice echoed, "Dispatch, four-seventeen."

Chase picked up his mic. "Go ahead."

"Four-seventeen got in contact with Lloyd Many Tears. He said he'd be happy to meet with you. Wants to know when and where?"

Chase thought for a moment. "Tell him I'll come to his home. I should be there within an hour and a half."

"Ten–four, four-seventeen, he said he'd be waiting."

He placed the mic back on its bracket and headed out of the desolate area. Harmony sat in silence. Chase wondered what she was thinking about.

His mind wandered to the many questions he would ask Lloyd, but he feared the answers more. Time was of the essence for the people on the reservation. He prayed he'd catch the murderer before any more victims turned up.

*****

He turned the knob on the radio, turning it up when the song he felt in his heart was his and Harmony's song.

"What do you think of this song? Its by Dan plus Shay."

She shrugged. "I haven't really heard if before."

"It's called 'From the Ground Up'"

She smiled as she heard the part:

 'Someday we'll wake up with thousands of pictures
Of 65 years in this little house
I won't trade for nothing the life that we built
I'll kiss you goodnight and say, "I love you still."
"You know I want that more than anything,"

She leaned over and kissed him. Her heart fluttered inside her chest.

They turned into the entrance to Chase's house. It was a log home with a wraparound porch. Beautiful. The sun radiated the area, Burden baskets and dreamcatchers hung on the rustic porch.

"Okay you get in there and stay, please."

She nodded and climbed out of the patrol unit.

She stood on the porch and watched the Arizona dust swirl behind the unit. The warmth of the sun filled her heart. Her thoughts and prayers went with her man. She turned and walked into the empty house. Closing the door behind her.

Chase looked up into his rear view mirror, catching a glimpse of Harmony, walking into his house. *"It better become our house soon."*

The dust boiled from under the tires as he drove down the dusty road. His journey to Lloyd's would be a time to ponder about his life. He realized that the only woman he would ever love seemed so far away from his grasp. He would not lose her again.

"Creator, please guide me on this journey and provide me knowledge to keep the only woman I would ever love. She is my heart. Also, guide me on my medicine journey to protect my people."

He placed his hand on the medicine pouch that hung around his neck. Soon, everything would come to him in a vision, which would guide him. Would it be enough to stop the murders and capture the woman who had his heart?

Chapter 6

Chase sat outside of the old, broken- down house. Most homes on the reservation weren't in much better shape.

He needed the help of Lloyd Many Tears for his cleansing. Lloyd sat on the porch, smoking his pipe. Chase stepped out of his patrol unit, walked up to the porch, and extended his hand to Lloyd. Silence stood between them as his granddaughter ran out the screen door.

"How old is she?" Chase blurted.

"She's four now. Strong- hearted. Her name is Teague," Lloyd said, pride puffing his chest.

"I need your help, Lloyd. Joe remains in the hospital and there is evil magic on the reservation. It's being used to kill more and more of our people. Would you be willing to help cleanse my soul, so I can face the dark magic?"

Lloyd walked over to the steps, leaning against the wooden post. "You're learning the medicine way, so I'll be honored in assisting you. I will need to gather some ceremonial items, and then we'll head out to Oak Flats."

Chase nodded and returned to his patrol unit. He was off duty now, and it was time to cleanse his soul. Lloyd gathered his last- minute items. Soon Chase would be prepared for the evil magic and be closer to catching the killer.

$$*****$$

Chase and Lloyd sat in silence. The drive to Oak Flat was one of importance. Chase realized his ancestors were there and would help guide him to the killer. He had to prepare for the battle.

"The scenery never gets old."

Chase nodded. "Yeah, the boulders are beautiful reaching to the sky. Our ancestors picked a beautiful place to live. Apache

Leap is really a sacred place. The warriors who leaped to their deaths are proof of the way we are brought up."

Lloyd reached into his handbag, which carried his sacred items. The rattle he brought forth reveal the turtle, which is Mother Earth. He began to shake it gently.

The chant followed which offered blessings to the spirits. A butterfly held onto the windshield. The legend goes that if you want a wish to come true then find a butterfly but do not touch its fragile features, and whisper your wish to it. Now, remember a butterfly cannot speak or make a sound so cannot tell the wish to anybody except the Great Spirit. Since the butterfly has its freedom, the wish will be taken to Heaven and granted.

"Lloyd, look a butterfly travels with us."

"Oh, this is a great sign. Make a wish, Chase and it will be granted."

Chase felt his heart flutter as he whispered his wish.

"Please Great Spirit, guide me to the killer and protect Harmony. Let us become a family."

Lloyd continued with the chant as they pulled into Oak Flats. It was quiet and surreal. Only the spirits of the ancestors roamed the area. Soon, Chase would become one with them.

*****

Chase sat in his patrol unit, watching the sunset, as Lloyd prepared the site. The marvels of reds, blues, and purples transported him to another plane of existence. The silence of his Native American ancestors roamed the area of Oak Flats. He wondered if his friend, the red–tailed hawk, would come for a visit.

Chase stepped out of his unit. Because of the presence of his ancestors, the place he went to pray was sacred.

The thunder of hooves rose to a roar. A herd of wild horses galloped closed by, the dust they raised stinging his eyes.

"Come," Lloyd, instructed. "Everything is ready."

He stood at the sacred spot. The ceremony was about to begin.

"Chase, you came to me and asked for your body to be cleansed from the dark witchcraft surrounding you. The time is here. Let us begin."

Chase followed the medicine man's every word, sitting on top of the most sacred place known to his people.

A blanket held all the items the medicine man would need. The smudge stick of sage, desert harmony, and sweet grass.

"Stand facing me. I've chosen to use the smudge stick today. One is made of desert Harmony, which will drive away negative energy, and the other is sweet grass, which is the most sacred of all our herbs because it brings positive energy once the negative energy has been expelled."

Lloyd bent and picked up the smudge stick and lit it. Once it was smoldering, Lloyd smothered it, sending the smoke into Mother Earth.

"Close your eyes, Chase, and listen to my words."

Chase faced the medicine man. He channeled his faith into him and the ancient ceremony. The medicine man chanted as he passed the smudge stick, starting at Chase's feet and moving upward, taking special note of the heart area before he continued to the head. Then the medicine man had Chase turn clockwise while he passed the stick down his back. Once completed, he repeated the ceremony with the Sweet Grass so positive energy would arrive.

"This blessing, *goch'ital,* ceremony, will help to guide you. The *ch'iin,* evil spirits, will release you now. Your mind is clear. Your *niyi' siziini,* your soul, is now free. You have renewed energy and knowledge. Walk your path strong."

To finish the ceremony, Lloyd pulled out his corn pollen. "Chase, *nohwik'I daidilta',* I sprinkle this corn pollen on you with the strongest of medicine. You shall find your way. Your mind is clear and strong. Help our people. It is in your hands."

Chase opened his eyes and nodded at Lloyd. He felt the presence of his ancestor, *Goyaale,* Geronimo. "Thank you."

Suddenly, he heard screeching noise in the sky, he looked up and saw his friend the hawk. This is a good omen.

With those words, Chase turned and climbed off the rock and headed deeper into Oak Flats, leaving Lloyd until he returned the next day. He would now seek guidance from his ancestors, whose spirits remained.

Every year he came to Oak Flats bringing blessings and prayers for his people. Lately, he found himself coming more often. His people lived in fear. His people lived in turmoil.

Chase approached the spot most sacred to him. His heart raced. He stopped and sat cross-legged, and offered the spirits many blessings. He hoped to learn why the killings seemed connected to his friend and mentor, Joe.

The sun slipped behind the mountains as Chase felt his ancestors dancing around him. His inner soul was now entering the phase of the vision quest. He removed his medicine bag from his pocket and slipped it around his neck. Chase placed his special items, which consisted of amulets of his spirit animal, the hawk, and sage, around him. The elements between Chase, his ancestors, and the animals were interconnected.

The quiet night surrounded him. The animals of the wild lurked, watching his every move. Chase sat in silence among the night stars. Chase waited for the red-tailed hawk, Guardian of Mother Earth, to arrive in his vision. He'd had a connection to the red-tailed hawk from an early age. The hawk had always been a part of his life.

Chase's vision began. Standing before him were his father and grandfather. It was as if it were a dream. His heart felt the warmth of his father, but he could not get close.

His father spoke first. "Chase, my son, you are of the red-tailed hawk people. You have a flair for life and are always hungry for knowledge. You are the element of fire. Passionate about every task you take on, even the murders. You are fearless, but a word of caution is warranted because you tend to react before you think and this could cause you problems. You cannot lie well, for it makes you sick to do so. Some people do not like your tactics, for you are honest and will tell the truth no matter whom it hurts. This is why you struggle. You must first be honest about your love for Harmony and seek the truth about your family. When you do so, everything else will come full circle."

Then the words and figures faded, leaving only the spirit of the greatest warrior of the Apache, *Goyaale,* Geronimo. He stood proud and fearless.

Blood tainted his clothing, and he spoke in his native tongue, saying, "Time has come for all Apaches to band together and stop the wrongs to our people. Then, and only then, will peace and harmony come full circle. You follow in my footsteps. You will be the next leader and medicine man for our people. Speak my name when times are hard, walk the red road, and then you will find answers to many questions.."

Chase jolted awake. His surroundings were vague. He glanced around, taking in the silence of the night, except for the wolf howling in the distance as the moon hung low, sending an array of spirits circling around him. It was true: he was of the red-tailed hawk people. He had the power to seek the answers through his visions.

Fatigue consumed him. Darkness filled the void.

*****

Morning came with enchanting songs from the beautiful Song Sparrow flying in and out of the trees, which covered the land. The beauty their songs released was overwhelming. Chase sat on the mound of rocks, recalling the vision's meaning. He was of the red-tailed hawk people. His eyes feasted upon the beauty of his land and the many animals that shared it with his people.

Chase jerked his head around, taking note as the red-tailed hawk swooped down and landed on the rocks within his reach.

"My friend, deelicho, hawk, you are one with me. You came to visit me with many warnings. I still must figure out your message. I know I'm of the red-tailed hawk people, your people. I have the ability to see more, do more, and interpret more than normal. I welcome you into my life. Guide me on the right path, my spiritual guide."

Then the hawk turned its head, revealing the strength of his beak and talons, stretched out its wings and swooped them in an upward motion, and lifted off in fight. The shrillness of its voice echoed through the canyon, sending the sacredness of the Apache People to a renewal of life. Chase stood, stretched his legs and breathed the freshness of the new day. His life was back on track. He was focused. Now to find the killer among his people was the hardest task he would ever encounter, but he would do his job no matter what it meant for his heart.

✶✶✶✶✶

Chase headed back to speak to Lloyd. He would offer insight to what his vision meant. He walked past the deep canyons and twisted ravines. As he approached, he notices Lloyd sitting on a high rock.

He reached and grasps the protruding rocks and pulled himself up. Feeling a sense of pride as he sat down beside this medicine man.

"I had the vision that I am of the hawk people. What does this truly mean? I know I am connect to this winged animal and I am so proud. But can you offer more insight?"

Lloyd sat quietly and turned as the hawk swooped through. "Yes, my friend you are of the hawk people. You have a greater significance here on earth. You will teach and lead the people. You will be their medicine man and you will protect us for a very long time. When you go to the spirit world, you will be one that is revered. Only you will be able to determine what is right and wrong. You will be guided by the hawk spirit people of long ago. Follow their lead and you will always be on the red road."

Chase's hands shook and he rubbed his head. "What, are you sure?"

Lloyd stood, "The spirits have spoken. This is your road...your path."

Chase followed Lloyd as they climbed off the rock. His mind spiraled out of control. He was the person to lead his people. He would be their medicine man. He walked proudly. He would make his ancestors and spirit guides proud, especially the hawk spirited people.

Chapter 7

Harmony drove down the winding curves to Joe's house, aware the engine light had come on again. She needed to pack some clothes and was sure she could get back before Chase came home. The scenery never failed to astound her. Statues sat along the dirt road leading to the log home, with many Apache accents along the way.

She pulled into the circular driveway, stepped out of her truck, and walked to the porch. An uneasy feeling followed her. Burden baskets lined the porch, clicking out a warning. Out, of the corner of her eye, she saw Ralan standing by the barn, glaring at her. She forced herself to remain calm. She stooped to remove the key from under the doormat and shoved it into the lock. It jammed. Her hands shook, and her heartbeat thumped in her throat.

The crunch of sand pebbles toppled behind her, not the continuous noise that comes from a rolling car, but the defined long grind of a footstep. Harmony fought the urge to turn and face Ralan. Then another scuff of a boot striking the pebbles, this time it was heavier and faster as if he wanted to warn me he was coming.

Ralan stalked toward her. Harmony's heart raced. Why had she come here alone? She took a deep breath. She would not succumb to her fear. She glanced in his direction. He picked up his pace. A surge of relief swept through her when finally, the key turned and the door opened. She rushed inside, and locked the door behind her. Breathless, she leaned against it. Ralan pounded on the door. Harmony's heart jumped to her throat.

"What are you doing in my father's house? You have no right to be here." His gruff voice echoed through the glass window.

Harmony opened the curtains. The burly man stood outside the door.

"I'm leaving, Ralan. I need to pick up a couple of things."

"Get out! You do not belong here." The doorknob rattled again.

Harmony stepped away from the door, her hand at her throat. She held her breath. His boots stomped down the steps, curses flying from his mouth. With a heavy sigh, she released her breath. *What would happen if Ralan got hold of her*, or gained entry into the house?

She took the steps two at a time to the top of the stairs to her bedroom. She cried in dismay at the mess she discovered as she opened the door to her room.

"Oh, my God!" A large pile of shredded clothing and ripped books lay on her bed. It must have been Ralan. She fingered what remained of her favorite blouse, a gift from her grandmother. Nothing had been spared. She felt violated. He had crossed the line.

She threw the tattered blouse to the floor and ran screaming down the stairs as she slammed the front door open. Fear vanished. Anger consumed her. She ran as fast as her legs would carry her to the barn. Birds tweeted in the nearby trees and the sun sent rays of warmth against her skin. Her rage blinded her. She flung the barn door open. Ralan stood brushing the horse, an evil smile on his face.

"What the hell do you think you're doing? You have no right going into my room and destroying my stuff!"

Ralan stopped brushing the painted pony and turned to stare into her eyes, "I don't know what you're talking about. By all means, please inform me of what I've done to make you so upset." The proud grin induced her anger even more.

"You will pay for this. I'm calling the cops."

Harmony turned to exit the barn. A steely hand wrapped around her waist. "You're going to do what?"

Ralan pushed her up against the barn door. Rusty nails ripped her shirt, and scratched her shoulder.

"Let me go! You're hurting me!" Harmony's fears mounted. Ralan was a strong man. His breath lingered on her neck. Her stomach clenched.

Several of the ranch hands heard her screams and came running, but only one spoke up.

"Ma'am, can I help you? Are you okay?"

Ralan released his hold, eyeing the men that defied him. Without a word, he left the barn and headed up the trail to his own small quarters.

The tall, muscular man resembled Chase, but it couldn't be. Her rescuer wore no shirt, only dirty boots and western jeans. Tight-fitting, faded jeans.

"Thank you," Harmony said, smiling as the young Apache man walked away. He nodded, his waist-length braid swaying. By the time she came out of the barn, the man with the mysterious smile had disappeared. *Who was the man who resembled Chase so much? She could not wait to tell him about this mystery. He would not believe it.*

Fearing Ralan would return, she hurried back to the main house. She ran up the flight of stairs, catching her breath on the landing before entering her room. She gathered what few things Ralan hadn't destroyed and shoved them into a suitcase, then sprinted down the stairs. She wanted out of there. Harmony opened the door and when she turned to replace the key under the mat, Ralan's evil smile met her from across the porch. He eased back into the chair.

Ralan wiped the sweat from his brow. "You are one pretty woman, Harmony Wind Dancer, and also very nosy. You best watch your step around these parts," Ralan grunted.

Harmony couldn't stand his atrocious ways. "What's wrong with you? You're Joe's son. Yet you're nothing like him."

Ralan jumped to his feet, trembling. "Yes, unfortunately I am. That part of me died with my mother. She was the only good thing in this world."

Harmony staggered with the potent force of his anger. The disturbed man's resentment of his father was palpable. She felt sick with the power of his hatred. Ralan turned and bounded off the porch, knocking against her with such force, he shoved her down the steps. She landed on her knees in the dirt, and so did her camera.

She bounced to her feet. "Ralan, what is your damn problem?" Harmony shouted as he disappeared into the barn.

Harmony wiped the dirt off her jeans. She snatched her suitcase and hurried toward her truck. As she placed it in the back, she noticed the young Apache watching her from behind a tree. *He looks so much like Chase.* Once he noticed Harmony gazing at him, he turned and disappeared into the distance. His watchful eye unnerved her. *Who was he? And what did he want?*

Harmony returned to the porch to make sure the door was secured. The heat of someone's gaze prickled her skin. Ralan, no doubt. Unlike his father Joe, he was angry and disturbed. She leaned against the pole, peering out over the large, desolate ranch. The sun lingered in the sky, setting off rays of colors over the desert. Her thoughts settled on Ralan's resentment of his father. *Was she onto something?*

Harmony picked her camera up from the ground where she had dropped it after Ralan had pushed her, and snapped as many pictures of Ralan and the strange, young ranch hand as she could. The men were hiding in separate places, watching her.

Yes, the pictures will prove to Chase that there was a mystery man who saved her from the hands of Ralan. The different angles of each of them would reveal who this man was. He looked so much like Chase. Who could he be?

Harmony climbed into her truck and turned the ignition. Nothing. *She knew the engine light would kick her butt sooner or later. Why now of all times?*

"This stupid piece of junk!" She pounded her fist onto the steering wheel.

Ralan approached the truck. She reached and slapped the lock. Her mouth went dry. She turned the ignition again... Nothing.

"Open the door, bitch!" Ralan jerked on the door handle.

Harmony glimpsed in his direction, turned and tried the truck again. Realizing she was going to have to face him, she turned back with a stern face, but he was gone.

Dust boiled from a vehicle flying down the dirt road. Harmony prayed it was Chase, despite the fact he would be furious with her for not listening to him. Her breath returned to normal as she feasted her eyes on the familiar vehicle. Ralan disappeared in the nearby trees, not wanting to face Chase.

She smiled when he slammed on his breaks. Dust rolled into a large cloud around them, and she gently raised her hand and waved. Chase had a tendency to get upset when he thought her life was endangered. Just like any man who loves his stubborn woman.

Harmony couldn't take her eyes off Chase. She was coming to terms with the power of her love for this man. Even though she'd promised herself she would not love him, she knew that promise to be weak. He was the center of her life. Repeatedly, she would find herself in the world of *Chase*. The forcefulness of his nature sent chills through her and the sparks from his dark– brown eyes heated her to the point of boiling, but she wasn't ready to admit that just yet–certainly not to him.

Harmony waited nervously for him to step out of his patrol unit. He stared at her through the dirty windshield. He grasped the steering wheel.

Chase stepped out of the patrol unit.

Harmony jumped from the vehicle and ran to Chase's arms. She was trembling all over. The hold was so tight he could was at a loss for words.

She pulled away and stared into his eyes. He felt only love for her but he had to stand firm. He had to make her understand her life was in danger and she had to stop doing things that jeopardized herself.

"Harmony, what the hell are you doing? You were to stay put?"

"Chase, I'm sorry, but I didn't think it would be a problem."

The vein in Chase's neck flared. "Let's head home. We'll discuss it there."

She smiled and headed back to her truck. Chase stomped back to his unit.

"Chase the truck won't crack?"

"Just try it."

The truck started as if Chase was the miracle she needed. *Wow, how come it worked just fine now?*

When would she tell him about Ralan and his temper? More importantly, when would she mention the young Apache man who'd saved her from the wicked hands of her aggressor, resembled him to the point he looked like a twin, but had also watched her every move?

Chapter 8

Chase watched Harmony on the couch, her legs crossed and working on a cradleboard, the skills handed down from her grandmother who'd taught her the Apache Way of life. He sat by the fireplace and turned to stare out the window. Mountains protruded out of the land, soaring toward the sky. The clouds resembled cotton balls floating effortlessly.

The silence between them increased to a deafening roar. He should have controlled his anger, but damn it, when you love somebody, fear overtakes your better judgment. He turned his focus on her. "Harmony, I'm sorry for exploding at you earlier, but you should not have gone to Joe's by yourself."

Harmony reached for a piece of the mesquite tree used in making the cradleboard. "I'm fully capable of taking care of myself. My grandmother taught me well."

Chase returned his gaze to the mountains. He wanted her to need him. Could he tell her that? NO, not now, with so much still unspoken between them; so he changed the subject. "So tell me, why did you decide to make the *me' bits'al,* cradleboard?"

"My grandmother taught me trees are like lessons in life, just like the *me' bits' al,* cradleboard. She explained that lessons of life cling to the leaves of the trees. If you listen, they will speak to you, just as they did to our ancestors. The making of the cradleboard holds a purpose. It adheres to all the exclusive attributes we all want our children to have."

Chase smiled, enjoying the crackle and warmth of the fire from the hearth. It was *daa,* Spring, so evenings could be cool.

"Please go on." He loved hearing her talk about walking the red road, which most find difficult to do.

"Well, in the months of *T'aa'nachil,* April, and *t'aa'nacho,* May, which are the months of *It'aa Nachoh, or,* leaves are full-grown. This is the best time to make the cradleboards. My grandmother told me that the frame is made out of the mesquite roots. The mesquite tree becomes soft in water so you can bend it into shape.

Then as it gets hard, it remains that way." She glanced at Chase and smiled. "Unless you need to bend it again. If so, then you make it wet and it will bend. Grandmother told me that is the way you want your children to grow so that they can bend with whatever comes their way."

Harmony paused and reached for some of the Yucca, her voice deep and strong with belief in what she shared. "Then you make the backboard, out of the Yucca." She held a piece up.

"The slats are made from Yucca. This plant grows straight and tall, which is, of course, what every parent wants their child to be: proud, straight, and tall."

As she spoke, Chase admired her high cheekbones, long brownish-black straight hair, and eyes dark as the night. She was beautiful in every way–inside and out. Watching her relaxed him as he sat on the chair with the designs of the hawk and wolf engraved on the wooden arms. He smiled at her. "Please continue."

Harmony picked up pieces of the willow tree. "The willow tree is used for the hood that goes around the baby's head to protect it. Grandmother explained that this is used so the child will grow strong and be grounded. Like the willow tree, the child will be able to bend and go with whatever life brings."

Harmony stopped and leaned back on the couch. "The cradleboard is important to our people, and I want my children to use the cradleboard so they are strong and rooted in traditions."

He reached out and took her hand. "I hope it is our children."

Just as Harmony was about to reply, the phone rang.

He stood and walked to the desk to answer the phone. "Hello." As he listened to the officer's grim news, he glanced at Harmony. Hands still, she watched him intently.

"Okay, thanks. I'll be en route in a couple of minutes." Chase laid the receiver back down. "I have to go. They've found another body. Don't you dare go out until I return." Then, remembering how she hated his telling her what to do, he softened his voice. "Please, Harmony. Knowing you're here, safe, will help me focus on my job. I'm going to stop by and have a talk with Ralan before I return."

"Why can't I go along?"

"Because you'll be a distraction."

Her irritated sigh expressed her displeasure. He reached for his gun, and, holstered it into the side of his boot, and turned to leave. He stopped and walked toward Harmony. With his hand under her chin, he titled her face upward until their gazes locked. "I meant, you'd be a beautiful distraction." Before she complained, he bent down and placed a kiss on her lips. Gentle sips at first to taste her; then he angled his head to deepen the kiss.

When he pulled back, her eyes were glazed and she couldn't speak. He relished her reaction, and wondered if she could see the passion that burned in his eyes.

He hurried outside and down the steps. Just as he thought he was in the clear with her, she was standing on the porch. "We'll talk when you return." Her arms were folded across her chest and annoyance replaced the passion he'd seen earlier in her eyes.

Chase opened the truck door and smiled. "Sounds good to me," he said, turning the ignition.

He pulled out of the circular driveway and headed down the long dirt road. As he reached the stop sign, a raven perched itself on the mesquite tree. A smile graced his face. The raven was a sign of goodness, a sign of protection. The power of the raven could counteract bad spirits like the owl. With the protection of the raven, Chase was more at ease leaving Harmony alone.

✶ ✶ ✶ ✶ ✶

Chase drove to the area of Bylas, the drive seemed to take forever. Another murder, but out of the area of the previous ones. According to the officer on the phone, the same beads were left at the scene near the victim. After he turned onto Deer Springs Road, the ride got rougher. It was graveled but with potholes. The road abruptly turned into dirt with huge holes that could beat a car's undercarriage. As his vehicle slowly bounced along, Chase came to the conclusion that the killer had to have a truck to navigate this uneven, scarred road. Finally, the other patrol unit came into view.

Chase pulled up and jumped out quickly to get to the scene. He scanned the surrounding mountains, and headed down the embankment guided by the voices echoing off the canyon walls. He rounded a large boulder. A hawk flew in his path. This was a warning of danger. His sharp vision scanned the area, as he thanked the hawk for the forewarning.

Chase continued down the rough terrain until he came to the body and the yellow tape strung around the boulders where it lay. The scene was the same. The deceased was lying on his back with the string of beads a few feet away. The body appeared to have been there for a short while. It was another middle–aged medicine man-John Pale Crest. Though John was a loner, everyone knew him.

Chase examined the corpse and found the man's wallet tucked into his back pocket. As in the other cases, robbery was not the motive. Chase searched for any signs of paintings, and there, on the nearby rocks, was the etched sign of death. The sun beamed down on the crime scene. A flock of buzzards flew overhead, and he cupped his hand over his brow to see. Some kind of problem was forthcoming. The buzzards circled overhead. Chase reached into his pocket and offered them some tobacco. He prayed, and offered them some more tobacco.

"Chase, it's the same as all the other murders," Officer Begay offered.

"It appears so. Were you the first on the scene?"

"Yeah, the only thing different is there was no fire to mark the location. So, he is resorting to fire with some but not with others."

Chase nodded. "You're right. So what does that mean? The flock of buzzards flew closer, and one swooped down and squawked loudly. It landed on a nearby jagged rock, beckoning Chase to follow. Near the rocks, a key glinted in the sun. As he neared, he noticed boot prints. His heart rate quickened. The killer had been lax in covering his tracks. Had the killer figured he was invincible? Or had he left in a hurry?

The hard part would be finding where the key belonged or its owner. Chase opened his medicine bag and offered the buzzard another bite of tobacco, thanking him for the clue. He pulled a plastic evidence bag from his pocket and deposited the key with a gloved hand.

Chase headed back to the body. It was his duty to say a prayer for the deceased and offer tobacco to the spirits. This is a way to open the door to the spirit world and let our loved ones cross over.

He bent down on his knees holding his medicine bag tightly. He took some pollen and sprinkled himself and the ground with it. Turning his head upward toward the sky and closing his eyes, he recited words of respect.

"*Ba oshkaahi,* my prayers for the victims." He placed his hand on the deceased man. "Keep their families strong and let them know that they did not die in vain. Please let them walk with our ancestors in the spirit world. Creator, protect our people."

Then Chase opened his eyes and sprinkled pollen on the deceased medicine man, and upon Mother Earth. He hoped to bring closure to the family and blessed the body. He turned full circle, releasing the spirit and blessing him on his journey into the spirit world.

His thoughts turned to the key. What did it go to? Could it solve the mystery and stop the murders? Did the deceased man pull it from the killer? So many unanswered questions. Chase walked to his patrol unit. He sat in the middle of the hot, scorching desert, wondering how his life had changed so much.

The key held the answer. It looked like a house key. Whose house? Hopefully, there would be fingerprints on the key that could be lifted. Why would anybody want to kill anybody, especially a medicine man?

Chase grasped his medicine pouch..."*Creator, please guide me on this path and help me to deliver my people from this evil.*"

Chapter 9

Chase drove in silence down Highway sixty, just past Top of the World. Oak Flats would be to the left. Tall trees made the area more serene. Chase focused on the place where the sacred sweat lodge ceremonies occurred. The ashes from the sacred ceremony remained on the ground in a circular mound. Casting his eyes around the area brought him peace. To the right of the ceremonial site was a smoke tree. From a distance, it resembled a puff of smoke. To the left of the smoke tree was the Indian Pipe.

Chase eased the truck into park, wiping sweat from his brow. Prayer was a part of the Apache way. Chase needed to speak to Ralan, so he came to Oak Flats to pray for guidance.

Chase climbed out of the truck, stretched his legs. He faced the sun and started his prayer. *"Usen, I have come to ask for guidance. Protect us from evil"* Then he began the long climb to his sacred spot. A place he traveled to often now so he could pray to the Creator, where his prayers would be answered.

The steep incline made it difficult to gain his footage. With each shaky step, loose gravel and dust rained into the canyon below. Finally, he made it to the first leveled area. The beauty of the Desert Willow stopped him in his tracks. It was an amazing tree. Its heart shaped leaves and flowers were pink. Chase recalled being taught to use the willow to make bows, and his grandmother made baskets from strips of bark from the tree.

In the distance, the Arizona walnut tree loomed toward Chase. His grandmother gathered the seeds of this tree. He shook the memories of his childhood from his mind.

Chase continued to climb the steep canyons and washes until he reached his final sacred spot. Surrounding it was the Pinyon Pine. Its leaves were needle-like but different, because two needles resided in each of its bundles. Many times, he used it to make medicine and to waterproof baskets.

The sacred spot Chase cherished so much had been used by his grandfather and father. The rock ledge hung underneath a big pine tree. Its branches covered the important place where his ancestors had roamed.

Chase sat cross-legged on the rock. He held his sacred bundle in his hand to help pray to *Usen*, God.   He closed his eyes, raised his arms toward the sky, and began the chant for the spirits to help him with his quest. He prayed for hours, waiting for a sign. Just as he was about to perform another ceremony to help bring the spirits to him, a quivering sensation touched his arm. Opening his eyes, a butterfly floated by.

The butterfly was a very spiritual animal. It represented the presence of good spirits. Chase reached to touch it, an ancestor spirit, which had come to guide him. The Painted Crescent's wings fluttered as it angled its way to land on his arm. Its gentle wing movements were elegant and graceful, its spots vivid yellow and white.

"You have come to guide me today. I need good spirits to show me what lies ahead. Thank you, dear ancestor, for taking the time."

Chase's eyes followed the butterfly until it was out of view. This made him think of what his grandfather had told him about the moth as they sat on the porch one evening when Chase was just ten. It was an insect and it, too, was a messenger from the spirit world." You must watch the moth to see if it delivers a warning," his grandfather had said. "If it lands on you and keeps following you around, then it's a messenger from a ghost." Chase chuckled. The story had scared him as a child. The words were as clear as if spoken yesterday.

"*Son, a good ghost will make you feel warm, but a bad ghost will make you get cold.*" Chase shivered. But there is a way to get rid of the ghost by using the smudge ceremony and asking the good spirits to take all the bad ghosts away.

His vision was over. The butterfly confirmed that good spirits surrounded him and they would guide him on this long journey. He slowly rose from the sacred spot. The beauty of Oak Flats was never ending. Towering mountains protruded from the earth, with patches of green brush enveloping the area. Many water holes of long ago lingered still today. Chase's ancestors had drunk from them on their journey many winters before his time.

As he turned to travel the sacred path, he noticed a huge rock balancing on the edge of the mountain. He continued on his way to the creek bed, where the ancestors had built a fort. Chase climbed to the top of the powerful boulders that protruded from the earth. He paused to take in the breathtaking scenery,

He made his last descent down into the parking lot of Oak Flats, climbed into his truck, and his journey was now clearer. As the engine roared to life, the sacred site in the rearview mirror caught his breath. Many spirits walked their path on this holy ground.

The sky was a picture painted on canvas with an array of radiant colors, blues, purples, and splashes of mauves. Picket Post Mountain rose in the distance; its shadows covered the area like a blanket.

Chase felt the presence of his grandfather and father while at Oak Flats. Numerous companies had tried to take Oak Flats from the Apache People, but Chase vowed that he would never let it happen. It was a promise made long ago, a promise he would keep. The Apache People considered Oak Flats sacred. Others could not see its importance.

The drive back through Globe was a daunting task. The town had grown over the last twenty years. The sign stated, *"You are now entering Apache Reservation."* Chase chuckled as he thought of the myths the reservation was known for. Soon he would be coming face to face with Ralan Spirit Eyes, a troubled man, but one who brought back a sense of pride for the Apache. He helped take care of the animals, especially the wild horses that roamed the rez.

Chase felt there was more to Ralan Spirit Eyes' troubles, and hoped a background check would reveal something they had missed. Ralan had moved off the rez, then returned without notice. Whatever secrets Ralan held, Chase vowed to find them; he would not stop until the truth was known. He just prayed that Joe Spirit Eyes, Ralan's father, would recover from his serious injuries.

He passed the casino, uneasy about the upcoming confrontation with Ralan. He was a difficult man to talk to. A loner, with no one he called a friend.

Chase felt the presence of evil witchery, but he also felt the existence of his ancestors, who stood with him. He would never give in to the evil. The good spirits would overcome the bad, but what would happen in the middle of the battle?

Chapter 10

Chase's mind filled with thoughts of *Inlgashn,* a person who bewitches, and *inigash nadaago'aa,* witchcraft, as he drove the winding, dirt road to Ralan's log cabin. Was witchcraft at work on the Apache Reservation? The cabin sat on the land close to his father's property. The long ride had given Chase time to think of the right words to say to Ralan. He did not want to come across too strong, but he had to prove his point. The deeper he went into the barren land, the emptier he felt.

"Spirits, please travel with me on this journey to face this strange man." Chase slammed on his brakes. The patrol unit slide sideways. His heart raced. At the entrance to the old log cabin sat an owl. Its eerie eyes focused on Chase. An odd feeling swept through his entire body. His stomach clenched. His breath came in short gasps.

"Only witches have the power to own an owl. What is going on?" Chase fixed on his surroundings, felt nauseated. The image of the many medicine man on the reservation, came to mind. He recalled the day a man was said to have used witchery on the tribal council. This was known to be true because if one possessed an owl, then he also possessed the powers of witchcraft. This would be forever in his mind, for the medicine man always knew who was using evil against his people.

He straightened the vehicle and headed to the parked truck sitting outside the log cabin. Refusing to take his eyes off the owl, he opened the car door and reached for the medicine bundle around his neck. Inside was his collection of protective amulets, cattail pollen, turquoise beads, and an eagle and hawk claws.

He gently shut the car door, not wanting to startle who or what was there, especially the owl for if the owl crossed your path it would bring death to the family or friends. Chase walked up to the front door and when he saw it was halfway open, he glanced inside and knocked. "Tribal police, anybody home?"

No response. Chase gently pushed the door open and stepped inside. His eyes widened at the mess. Scattered clothes, piles of dirty dishes, and the rancid smell of fish hung in the silence like a dirty pair of socks.

"Ralan, are you here?"

Silence...

Chase continued his walk-through. His hand rested on his sidearm when he noticed a closed door down the hallway. He approached it cautiously. A noise from the front of the house startled him. Drawing his gun from its holster, he ran toward what he'd heard, his footsteps light and stealthy. He rounded the entrance to the living room, the same time a cat sauntered by a pile of strewn magazines.

"Well, fellow, you are one lucky cat. I could have blown you away." Chase reached down and patted the cat on the head, taking note of its color-black-the color of witchcraft.

He turned and again approached the closed door at the end of the hall, wiping beads of sweat from his brow. The doorknob turned easily in his hand. Unlike the rest of the house, this room was immaculate. His boots squeaked as he made his way around the room, table after table of perfectly lined items-colored stones, animal bones, at least fifty different herbs, human hair, and numerous hawk and eagle feathers.

Chase's heart sank. Ralan was into witchcraft. This did not prove he was the killer, but Chase knew he had to keep an eye on him. He held his breath. The stale odor coming from the house nearly made him sick. But, medicine bundle around his neck gave him comfort as he turned to leave the room.

He stepped onto the porch and gulped large breaths of fresh air. The stench inside the room indicated witchery. The winds blew strong, easing the urge to retch. He leaned toward the railing, noting the large population of owls living here.

It hit him. He'd been squinting. The place was dark inside. He glanced back over his shoulder at the gloomy interior of the house, remembering how it made him feel; the spirits inside oppressed him, as if to smother him.

A horse whinnied. Chase jumped over the log post fence, ran around the building, and came face to face with Ralan Spirit

Eyes. The man stood mere inches from him, filthy and his clothes bloodied.

"Ralan! I've been waiting for you."

Ralan turned to him. "What do you want?" He scowled, "I don't have time to fool with you. Say what you came to say, and leave."

Chase wiped the back of his head, "I've come to check on you, but I also need to speak to you about Harmony Wind Dancer."

Ralan's scowl turned to a lecherous smile; "Oh, that good lookin' thing. What about her?"

Flames seared Chase's soul. He couldn't hold back. He grabbed Ralan's arm, twisted it behind his back, and took him to the ground, the disrespect for the woman he loved turning into an acrid taste in his mouth.

"Watch what you say about her. I came here to talk with you, not to fight, but when it comes to Harmony, you will show respect. Leave her alone. She's only doing her job. She's a news reporter, and she has the right to get the word to our people about the murders. Hell, Ralan, your own father lies in the hospital and may not make it. What the hell are you doing here? You should be with him."

Ralan's face turned red, and he pushed Chase off him. Both men stood, eyeing each other warily.

"You do not tell me what to do. My father is no concern of yours. And that pretty little thing, Harmony, sounds like you have something for this reporter." He grinned. "She's fair game. You have no claim to her. You had your chance."

Chase lunged, taking Ralan to the dirt. They each fought for control as their bodies rolled down the steep hill, dodging trees and tumbling over bushes. Each punch sent them closer to the lake at the end of the forest line and into the water. Chase hit his head. For a brief moment, blackness drowned him, but the cool water kept him conscious.

Ralan pulled him out of the water and slumped to the ground.

"What in the hell is the matter with you?" he said, panting for air. "I only speak the truth. What man would not think Harmony is not attractive?"

Chase gasped. Ralan was right. He pushed himself into a sitting position. "You're right man, but understand, she's mine. Never touch her again."

"Then tell her to stay off my property."

Chase had to get him focused on what was inside his house. He changed the subject.

"What are you doing with all the hair samples?"

Ralan tensed. "And what the hell are you doing, snooping around my house?"

"Where'd you get those samples?"

"What I have inside those walls is nobody's business."

"What about the owls that live here? *Inlgashn*, witches attract owls."

Several owls flew in front of Ralan. "This is my home and I can have what I want here. Now leave!" He turned his back to walk away.

Chase pushed himself off the ground, "Stay clear of Harmony."

As Chase walked away, he heard Ralan's muffled words but he continued toward his unit. He kept his eyes to the ground. He opened the door and climbed inside. He placed the key into the ignition, but hesitated, his keen eyes spotting a figure resembling an image of him. Ralan stood inches from the image, but pretended not to see it as Chase backed up to leave.

Was the sun playing tricks on him? The image of a man who looks like me was watching. What the hell, is going on here? It must be the evil that lurks here that is making me see things.

He rubbed his eye, trying to focus on the dirt road. What was going on in this evil house. Ralan is behind this in some way. What was it going to take for him to find the truth that Ralan Spirit Eyes was the killer?

Chapter 11

The drive back to Chase's ranch seemed surreal. Lost in a dreamlike state, he relived every exchange at Ralan Spirit Eyes' place. Evil dwelled there. Ralan was evil. Ralan also had his sick sights aimed at Harmony; for some reason, he wished her harm. He had to keep Harmony away from him, to protect her.

The patches of Peyote growing in several places on Ralan's property did not escape him. The plant's presence added to his unease. Medicine men used peyote, a hallucinogenic drug made from the peyote cactus, during ceremonies. Unfortunately it was also used by witches to bring harm to others. Acid rolled in his stomach as he accepted mentally what his spirit told him: Ralan was a witch. Now, he understood his demeanor. It represented black witchery. Chase's stomach churned. A string of Harmony's hair was all that was needed to cause her inner turmoil and outer pain.

The night sky crept slowly over the desert landscape. Numerous animals stalked many paths, hunting for their prey. Was Harmony Ralan's prey? She was in danger. It was no secret Ralan despised her.

A wolf howled in the moon–filled sky, taking Chase to another plane of existence. Was the image of the young man real? *The image favored me.* Ralan had been mere inches from him, yet he never acknowledged his presence. Was it just an apparition? A warning of what was to come?

Chase glanced into his rearview mirror. The release of the orange colors entwined with pink; eased his heart. That cherished oneness with the elements enveloped him. He focused on his Navajo ways alongside his Apache ways. He knew about the shapeshifters in Navajo lore, but now they had surfaced onto Apache land. Was the witchcraft so evil it materialized into the most evil of all? *Yee naaldlloshii*, Skin Walkers....

He began thinking and speaking in his, Navajo tongue while also using his Apache heritage. The serenity and strength of his

Native tongue poured into every cell of his being, quenching the thirst for who he was in his heart, in his soul, and in his blood. He gave thanks to his ancestors who had passed the knowledge and essence of walking the good red road to him many years ago. To walk the red way meant doing what the Creator has instructed you to do.

A grotesque figure appeared on the road directly in front of him. His heart stuttered. His pulsed raced. *Where had it come from?* He kept his eyes locked on the figure, and slowed to a stop a safe distance away.

The disposition of the seven-foot spirit was unearthly. Covered in hair, the creature had powerful arms hanging down its sides. Claws dangled from oversized hands, and sharp teeth gnashed in the fading sunlight.

The sight unnerved him. "What the hell?"

Chase's knuckles turned white from his fierce grip on the steering wheel. His heartbeat pounded in his ears. Was this a sign? A warning? The consequences to come if he pursued Ralan Spirit Eyes?

Determined not to show fear, Chase reached for the medicine bag hanging on his rearview mirror. It was gone. It held his charms, and could be used against him if a witch got hold of its contents. The witch would then be able to manipulate his mind. He would have to seek council with the elders and the medicine men. Only the strongest of medicine men would be able to help him.

Chase gunned it. Stones and dirt flew. The show of fear was not an option. The image of this unearthly creature would disappear as long as he held to his faith and drove straight through the mirage. He heard his grandfather's voice like an echo in his mind: *"My grandson, the mind can be tricked to see things that are not there. Show strength and you will prevail."* As he neared it, the figure disappeared just as his grandfather had predicted.

He stopped and glanced over his shoulder. How could he explain this to anyone? How could he explain it to the woman he loved? More importantly, how was he going to explain to Harmony about Ralan, his witchcraft, and the shapeshifters?

✶✶✶✶✶

Harmony paced the length of the living room, staring through the double–paned windows. *Where the hell is he?*

Repeated phone calls went straight to voice mail. Not unusual on the rez in normal circumstances, but these were not normal times and he had gone to visit Ralan. That man gave her the creeps. There was something unnatural about him. A strong foreboding twisted her stomach. Unable to continue the monotonous wait, she dialed the number for the police department dispatch.

"Tribal Police. How can I help you?"

"Could you get hold of Officer Spirit Walker and tell him I really need to speak to him?"

Silence encased the phone and the conversation. "Officer Spirit Walker is out on a call, but I'll give him the message."

Harmony tried to sound cheerful. "Okay. When you hear from him, please tell him to call me. I'm Harmony Wind Dancer."

"As soon as he checks back in, I'll give him the message."

"Thank you."

She laid the receiver down, turned toward the mountains. "Please, Creator, protect Chase. Evil reigns on Ralan Spirit Eyes."

She sat on the sofa, her heart in deep pain. She had to be strong. She could not allow fear to overtake her. These last few days, she'd come to realize how much she cared for Chase. She was happiest when she was with him, yet she feared their past troubles would overtake them again. There were also fears about Ralan and the murders. Sometimes Chase was too brave for his own good.

*****

Chase was nearly home when he remembered he had not informed dispatch that he'd left Ralan's residence.

He snatched the mic off its holder. "Dispatch, I will be ten-eight from Ralan's residence, have been for approximately forty-five minutes. Sorry. Forgot to tell you."

"Ten-Four, Please call Harmony Wind Dancer ASAP." The wispy voice replied.

"Copy, I will be ten-seven for the rest of the day."

"Copy, have a good evening, sir."

Chase hung the mic back up and wiped his head. Harmony was going to be so angry. He'd forgot to call her when he left Ralan's house, as he had promised. Now that he was nearly home, he decided it would be no use to call now.

The missing medicine bag haunted him. Pellets made from charms could be injected into him or placed around his home. If this were to happen, not only would it be difficult to catch the killer, but he could lose Harmony again. He'd been taught evil would follow him. His loved ones would shy away and wickedness would possess him.

He must tell her about what he'd seen at Ralan's, but he feared her reaction. He turned into his driveway, sensing the anger coming from her. There was nothing like making that woman furious. She seen things the way she saw them and nothing could change her mind. Still, the curse from a witch would be far more damaging than being chided by the woman he loved.

Chase climbed out from his vehicle. Harmony stood in the doorway anger on her face. The bright full moon hung in the sky, causing Chase to realize that spirits lived all around him most of the time. But if the shapeshifters followed him, he would have major problems.

Tomorrow, I will seek advice from the medicine men. They will know what to do....

When the explosion of her anger was over, he would tell her about the witchcraft at Ralan's house. He would also tell her of the possible curse placed on him and about the mysterious man at Ralan's. Chase prayed it would not scare her. He would protect her with his own life. No witchcraft would scare him away from what he loved. Not even the *yee naaldlooshii*, skin walkers. Chase would win this fight if he kept his faith and sought council with the elders and medicine men on the rez.

The witch would try everything to tear them apart. Was their love strong enough to endure? This alone was the most fearful thing that plagued his heart.

*****

"Where have you been? Why didn't you call me?"

"I will explain."

"Well I have been worried sick. All kinds of thoughts ran through my head."

He reached and grabbed her. "I am fine. I will explain, but for now let me hold you."

He felt her go limp in his arms. The night was creeping up on them. He took her by the hand.

"Let's look at the stars. Have you heard the story about the stars?"

"No, I don't think I have."

"I was told this many years ago as a young child, I hope I remember it, The there were reddish-orange lights that indicate the east and west. There are small stars that run down that is the Milky Way and some believe it is a pathway of dead spirits. To the left of the Milky Way are nine to ten stars and they call them the Council of Chiefs, and they watch over the people. Anyway, it went something like that."

"Wow, Chase that is really amazing."

"Well, again I'm not sure that is exactly that way it goes but it sure got your attention."

Harmony smiled. "You sure know how to get me to get all into you."

"That's my job. If you are focused on me then nothing else matters."

He turned to her. "I love you, Harmony. Don't ever forget that."

She placed her hand to his cheek. "As I love you Chase."

They hugged and the night ended with a hint of the coyote... howling in the distance.

The thought of the trickster made Chase tighten his grip on her.

"Are you okay Chase?"

"Yes, just want to hold you as tight as I can."

She leaned back into his arms, as she stared up into the heavens. Chase realized he would die to protect her. His heart quivered at the mere thought of something happening to her. NO, he would not allow it.

The night ended with them talking a stroll and staring at the sky. Chase would forever hold this night in his heart. He would use his guides to protect her. Would he be able to do it or was it just a prayer? All he knew was he would die trying.

Chapter 12

Chase grimaced. *Witchcraft.* The thought agitated him and he felt the fear Harmony would develop after he explained to her the full extent of the problems he was facing. The witchery way or corpse-poison way had claimed his rez. Whoever the witch hoped to scare....it was working.

"So, what's playing around in your mind?" Harmony quizzed.

"Come, take a seat." Chase patted the sofa. "We need to talk."

The warmth of the fireplace enveloped them as they gazed into each other's eyes.

"Chase, you're scaring me now. What's wrong?"

"I believe witchcraft is at work. It's the way of the Navajo, not the Apache side of me, the person's taught by their parent or grandparent. Witches use corpse poison. They get this from the fingerprints of deceased children. Once used, the person could fall victim to a disease, nothing can help him, not even a ceremony."

"What are you telling me? What are we going to do?" She cried.

"With me being half Apache/half Navajo this is very important for you to understand, and I will explain it to you."

Harmony nodded and he continued.

"The witches perform dark ceremonies. They gather in a secluded place, in their animal form. This is what we as Navajos call Shapeshifters. I don't believe it has reached this level yet, but they're working hard to bewitch me."

"Why would they try to do that to you? What in the hell is going on?"

Fierce eyes stopped her words. He grasped her arm. "The way they perform this is by taking something that belongs to me, whether it is clothing, fingernails, hair, or personal belongings, such as my medicine bag."

"Cha...."

Placing his finger to her lips, he went on, "Then it would be buried with the corpse flesh, and usually the bewitched person dies within four days. They can also use these objects to curse a person, using bone beads or they can use charms to induce emotions. The shapeshifters have supernatural abilities. Never underestimate them. Do you understand, Harmony?"

"Yes." Harmony swallowed feeling a lump in her throat.

"You must understand. I have to find a medicine man to perform the Enemy Way. This will disperse the evil and restore balance, but I may have to stay away from you for a while. Shapeshifters can alter the mind."

"So, with the Enemy Way it will protect you?"

"The Enemy Way is a ceremony, we as Navajos, perform to help aid in the encounter of the harmful effects against the witches or *chindi.* I will do this by using sand paintings, chant, and dance."

Harmony sank into the leather Broyhill recliner. Chase watched her stunned reaction, but knew he had to tell her everything.

"Harmony," he said, pausing. "I must travel deep into our sacred land. I must go into a sweat Hogan to deter the witchcraft at work against me. It can't be denied. They have my medicine bag."

"So that means what?" She asked. He saw the terror on her normally solemn features.

"They can use it to bring fear, hurt, and even death."

Tears cascaded down her cheeks. "You're in true danger. Are you sure it's not big foot that is doing this?"

"My fear is not for my safety, but yours. They'll aim for whom I love. No, it's not the mythical creature, Big Foot, so please stop asking me. I told you I see him in my visions but it's only a warning. Now back to what I was saying, while I'm gone, you must stay here, but not alone. Can someone you trust stay with you?"

Her temper flared. "I don't need anyone!"

He wrapped his arms around her trembling body as she eased back in the recliner.

"It will be okay; just remember to use caution."

Silence fell between them.

Chase's heart broke from the pain he was causing. He would protect her even if it meant his own demise.

"You look tired, so let's lay down and take a nap and empty our minds."

Harmony nodded. "I hope I can empty my mind and dream about something wonderful happening."

"Just think about us and this will bring good vibes to your dreams."

Chase prayed Harmony would survive this ordeal. It was taking a toll on her. His heart ached for her pain. He would be there to pick her up.

＊＊＊＊＊

Harmony tossed and turned. The skin walkers were after Chase. How could this be happening? She sat up in bed, turned to him, but he was gone. *Where is he?*

She jumped out of bed and headed down the hallway. She glanced into the kitchen; nothing. She walked over to the window and saw him standing on the porch, glancing at the mountains, sipping on coffee.

She stepped through the door and Chase turned to her.

"What are you doing up?" he asked frowning.

He wrapped a blanket around her. "I couldn't sleep. I have to share something with you, Chase."

His bewildered eyes focused on her.

"When I went to get my things at Joe's," she said slowly, I thought I saw an image. I figured it was my imagination playing with me."

His stomach knotted. "Oh, God... I saw one too, but go ahead."

Harmony cleared her throat. "Well, he looked like you, and that's why I thought it was my mind messing with me. It was as if he was watching out for me."

"I saw the same image. It was as if he was watching out for me too, and I thought he favored me. This is to strange because it was as if Ralan couldn't see it. He almost walked right through it!"

"Oh, Chase, that's how I felt! Ralan never even glanced his way. I have no idea what's going on but I am worried sick. If it's what you think, it could end everything we know."

He nodded. "Come, my love. Let's return to bed. I promise I'll protect you."

Harmony wrapped her arm around his waist and felt herself start to relax. She was in the arms of the man she loved and that was all she cared about.

$*****$

Chase edged on his elbow, as he watched Harmony sleep. The sandman had not come to visit him just yet. Listening to her soft moans, he laid his head back down. The thought of the look-alike image he'd seen resurfaced in his mind and now he knew that Harmony had also seen it. *What was going on?....dark witchcraft was closing in on the reservation.*

Chase drifted into a deep sleep. Swirls circled above his head. *Where am I?* He tried to move but he was dead weight. Then his father stood before him.

"My son, the truth will surface for you soon. Blame nobody for what you will learn. At the time it was the best decision for me to make. Your mother needs for you to understand. She's doing good here in the spirit world with me. She loves you. You must reveal fear because we walk with you in every situation."

Lights flashed. Thunder boomed. Chase jumped up and startled Harmony.

"Are you okay?"

"Sorry, just had a weird dream."

"Want to talk about it?"

"Well, it was my father. He said I'd learn something soon, not to blame anybody, and to accept that it was for the best. What's he trying to tell me?"

"Chase, I'm sure whatever it is, everything will turn out okay."

He slipped back into bed, wrapping his arms around his love. Silence encapsulated them, and sleep took over.

✳✳✳✳✳

The smell of coffee woke Chase. He sat up in bed. He realized that his woman was already up and working. He slipped on his robe and walked down the hallway to the kitchen.

"I thought you might want some breakfast before you left," she said, smiling.

Chase hugged her. "You are something else, you know that?"

He sat at the table and she placed his plate in front of him.

"Oh, wow! Eggs, bacon, toast, and even some acorn oatmeal. Boy, I must be special to somebody, huh?"

"Don't push your luck, but I guess you are."

Chase smiled and smacked her butt.

He wondered if she was okay or if she was pretending for his sake. He glanced over and she was staring at the mountains.

"Like to talk about it?"

Harmony chuckled. "I could never hide anything from you."

"Nope, and you never will."

"I was thinking about your dream and what it could mean? Your father's trying to prepare you for something."

"Harmony, please don't ponder on things that we aren't sure about. Whatever it is, I'll look at it with both eyes and handle it."

"I know you will, but it scares the hell out of me."

He kissed her. "So, let's spend some time together before I have to go. Maybe we can go for a walk and take in Mother Nature or whatever you would like to do."

She reached for his hand. "Let's take that walk out in the middle of nowhere. It will only be the animals and us. Maybe we will have a chance to do some things we haven't done in a long time."

He took her hand and they headed out. The sky offered a solitude for one with the Creator. He felt the shake of her hand. He knew in his heart that he would protect her no matter what but the expression on her face revealed that no matter what he told her, she would continue to worry. He understood the emotions she was feeling because he too felt an uneasiness that tugged hard at his heart.

*****

Crisp morning dew hung on the rooftops. Chase threw his bag onto the porch. He dreaded the goodbyes. His heart broke.

"Love, I will be back to you before you know it. Keep the doors locked and if you sense any trouble, call nine one one."

"I promise. Please be careful and know my heart will be with you. You're the best man I know. I regret the time we missed out on, but we'll make it up." She turned away, not wanting him to see the tears rushing down her face.

He wrapped his arms around her, as her tears broke into heavy sobs. "We will, I promise. I love you more than there are words."

"Oh, Chase I've always loved you. Please be careful and take care of yourself."

"I'll keep you locked in my heart until we're together again."

He placed a kiss on her lips and quickly turned and walked away. He climbed into the truck and turned the ignition. Glancing back at the porch, he caught her gaze. He blew kisses toward her and she caught them and whisked them back at him. The dirt floated up in the air as he drove away. He looked away not wanting to see her disappear as he drove away. Legend had it if you are driving away and you watch that person until they are completely out of sight, then they might not return. He had to return for she was his life.

His mind raced as he turned onto Highway Sixty. Mount Graham, erected in the distance, gave him a sudden burst of hope. His people depended on him, and he would not let them down. Harmony was his woman, and he would not let her down. The coyote sat on the side of the road. Chase stared at this animal, a trickster. *Who was going to try and trick him?* He wondered. The coyote was one that would trick the mind. He would appear as a friend, giving good advice, then he would snap you into. No, not this time. Chase would be prepared for the trickster.

His heart and mind would be pure and cleansed after the Enemy Way ceremony. He would learn the mysteries his father had warned him about. The fight against dark witchcraft would happen soon, and he would be prepared. Nothing would stop him.

Chapter 13

The sky calmed, but a storm brewed on the horizon. Grit from the dirt driveway stuck to his lips. Returning to Lloyd Many Tears meant a more intense ceremony would be performed.

The shaman's lone figure stepped off the porch, cradling all the items for a blessing.

"How could he have known?" Chase whispered.

Without acknowledging Chase's presence, Lloyd walked past the driver's door with an armful of blankets, special amulets, drums, and rattles, and deposited them in the sacred circle of the forked stick sweat Hogan. The forked poles stood covered in mud, brush, and logs, a place of sacredness that would purify the body and soul.

Stepping inside, Chase's senses enveloped his inner soul.

Balance...

Chase's body welcomed the purification and healing that this ceremony would provide.

Lloyd examined the surroundings inside the willow lodge, meticulously smudging every item into a state of purity. He stood around a mound of rocks placed in the center of the dwelling. Steam rose as the elder sprinkled water over the rocks. The rocks grew hot from the fire beneath.

Chase handed the elder a bundle full of sage. Chase relaxed as Lloyd accepted his gift. Soon his spirit would gain purity. He took a seat and his thoughts returned to Harmony. Performed by a Navajo medicine man, the Enemy Way ceremony would last a week. Though relieved the ritual would soon begin, Harmony's safety tugged at his heart.

Chase's thoughts returned to the present. *Had Lloyd sent for the medicine man that would travel from the Navajo Reservation? Would the ceremony begin soon? Who would travel from the Navajo Reservation to perform the ceremony? Would it be a relative of his from his father's family? Being half Navajo and half Apache led to an interesting life.*

The flap opened and Wendsler Spirit Walker stepped inside.

Chase's mind went blank. His heart raced and bile churned in his stomach. *Why had he come?*

As Lloyd approached, Chase rose slowly. The elder caught his eye. "Your uncle came to perform the Enemy Way."

Chase nodded, though anger filled his heart. Legs stiff and lips pursed, Chase attempted inner control.

"My brother's son, my heart's happy to see you. It's been many years."

Chase dislodged the anger and swallowed his pride. "That it has."

Wendsler turned to handle the task set before him. He failed his brother but this time around, he would be there for Chase.

Chase stepped through the doorway and waited outside the sweat hogan, wondering how many of his clan members would come too. The *Nidaa'*, Enemy Way, ceremony would start soon. The forked stick, Hogan, rose straight up, and immediately in front of it stood a small arbor made out of wood and brush. About fifty feet away, on the southwest side, a larger arbor stood, made out of wood and brush, serving as a cook shed.

The meeting night, the first night of the ceremony, always fell on a Monday. During this time donations were given, and talk of who would receive the ceremonial staff. This sacred piece, made from cedar and juniper, was decorated with yarns of many colors and adorned with eagle feathers.

"Come, Chase." Wendsler motioned.

Chase took note of his family members.

"It is time to eat and socialize," Wendsler declared.

"Yeah, I can see that," Chase mocked.

Chase mingled with his clan. The stories exchanged brought him back to the storytelling his father had often shared with him. His gut ached at the bitter memory of his loss. What had happened to his dad? The anger dwelled deep inside. *My uncle knows more than he is sharing.*

"So, Uncle, what have you been up to?"

"I've been busy. I joined the Navajo Rangers. We explore the paranormal."

"Sounds intriguing." Chase blocked his uncle's step. "Maybe I should check it out."

Wendsler stepped back. "I welcome your interest."

Chase's wary gaze fixed on his uncle. His fear grew at the thought of what his uncle knew of the truth surrounding his father's death. The tension inside him grew. Nothing would change until his uncle came clean.

"Chase, tomorrow your ceremony will begin," Lloyd announced.

Chase spun on the heels of his Justin boots. "Yes, sir, soon everything shall come forth and be revealed."

His keen eyes pierced through his uncle. Wendsler abruptly stopped picking up his charms and sage. His shoulders tightened.

Truth lies within my uncle. There is more to be learned.

Chase shook the restless thoughts from him mind. For the ceremony to work, his mind had to be free from all disruptions. For now, a clear mind was vital.

* * * * *

Sitting by the open fire, Chase sipped his tea, his mind slipping between bits of conversation and thoughts of Harmony. Was she safe? Thoughts of her warmed his heart. Soon this nightmare would end, and their lives could get back on track. Soon.

The thought relaxed him, but that time couldn't come fast enough.

Chapter 14

Harmony put the final changes on the article about Big Foot. In the last couple of years residents spoke, in grave detail, about the creature roaming the reservation. Her thoughts wandered. Could this be the killer Chase searched for? She had spoken to him on numerous occasions, asking if this could be the killer but he always stated no, even though he had visions of this creature.

Chase. She hit 'enter' and rested her chin in her palms. *He wouldn't allow me to go...Only clan members are permitted.*

The clock chimed midnight. Later today, the ceremony would begin. Her faith in Chase outweighed any doubt she harbored, or fear that lingered.

Harmony stretched with a wide yawn. Her misgivings tucked into the back of her mind, she rose and slipped quietly down the hallway. The sandman called her name.

* * * * *

Darkness enveloped her soul. The storm brewing inside her calmed, she relaxed.

Lying on her side, visions of comfort floated across her senses, the lone call of the wolf in the distance lulling her to sleep. She fell into an odd sleep where haunting eyes pierced her skin. She opened her eyes as cold hands grabbed her from her slumber. Her eyes flew open and in the sudden jolt of wakefulness, a tall dark figure loomed above her, forcing his strength against her to hold her down. Scratching and biting through his skin was the only way to deter her attacker.

Rough, calloused hands wrapped her hands and mouth with duct tape, hoisted her body over his shoulder and hauled her to a truck waiting outside.

Harmony's mind spun. Sheer terror raced through her and sickened her stomach....*What's happening?* Dizziness wrestled with consciousness, and all went black. Then her mind floated to Chase. *He would come and save her.* Everything went black.

✶ ✶ ✶ ✶ ✶

Unfocused eyes fluttered open. *Where was she?* Glancing in her attacker's direction, she didn't recognize him or his voice. Silence filled the empty space.

The sun crested over the horizon. She faced her assailant, trying hard to see past the beanie and black clothing. "What do you want with me?" Anger slowly replaced the fear. "Answer me!"

Squeaky brakes were the only response.

Words were useless. Facing the window, she stared at her surroundings. The place looked familiar. *Was this Cochise Stronghold? Where the horrible battle Cochise fought in 1862 against Colonel James Carlton at Apache Pass?* A battle for life. Like the one, she was now facing.

Mesquite trees dotted the land and large boulders littered the area. The fierce Chiricahua warriors once hid behind these boulders, waiting for the right moment to attack. The Dragoon Mountains, sacred to the Apache people, hid many mysteries. Would she ever see them again?

Abruptly the truck stopped. The stranger climbed out. Harmony's pulse raced. *Now what?*

Opening the passenger door, he grabbed her pajamas and yanked her to her feet. Rocks bruised and bloodied her bare feet.

"Cooperate and you'll be okay." The man's rough voice echoed through her.

"But what...."

"No questions." He removed the duct tape.

"Let me go! If you didn't want to hear my mouth, you should have kept the tape on."

Ignoring her, he dragged her toward an opening in the boulders and slammed her against them. She winced with pain, then kicked him as hard as she could with nothing more than an unprotected foot.

"Scream too, if you want. Nobody will hear you."

88

"You'll regret this, asshole."

His voice screamed of malevolence. "Shut up!"

She quieted down, not wanting the tape over her mouth again. The boulders obstructed the view of her surroundings. Harmony noticed the petroglyphs on the rock face. Elders of long ago roamed here. The gentle sounds of young birds calling out to their mother infused the area. The only sound was Brother Wind, whispering softly as if to create calmness.

The flat, dusty trail turned to rough, jagged rocks. Loose gravel plummeted to the ground below where death would fall to anybody who took a miscalculated step.

Harmony memorized every aspect of the trail. Yucca plants dotted the landscape. Her thoughts skipped to the time her grandmother had taught her about weaving baskets out of the yucca. Then the mesquite trees enveloped her sight. This was used to make *atole,* flour from the bean. Her people used it for cuts and abrasions.

Harmony sensed her ancestors. Finally, an opening inside the ground emerged. "NO! Please? Not here!"

Kicking at the cruel man only made him angrier.

"Stop it. You have food and water. All you need."

"What the hell is this all about?"

"He will come for you, and then he dies," the scruffy voice growled.

"No, Chase's heart is for our people."

Pointing to a rope ladder in the deep, dark hole, he motioned for her to go down. "Go. Don't make me force you. It will be easier if you obey."

She grabbed hold of the rope and started her descent. The dark, cold earth opened around her and she released a resigned breath as the ladder was pulled back to the surface.

"Please don't do this! Don't leave me here!"

A huge rock was placed over the hole. The intensity of her screams vanished as his lone set of footsteps faded into nothing. *"You will not win this battle,"* she thought. *"No way."*

✶✶✶✶✶

Harmony glanced around in the darkness. She'd seen a flashlight before the light had been sealed off by the rock. She fell to her knees, groped in the direction she remembered and patted a bedroll laid to the left by a pile of blankets. Her fingers closed around the flashlight. With one click of the button, light flooded the earthen room. Food and water lay up against the east wall and a stack of books lined the north. The room was cramped and dank. Her stomach turned. She beamed the light on the walls. A lone hand print along the east wall was a porthole to the spirit of a medicine man who had preceded her to these cramped quarters.

Grandfather taught me about the power of medicine men. If a person has the power to be a medicine man, or woman, then they can place their hand over the same handprint and communicate with the living spirit of the dead.

She placed her hand on the handprint of the medicine man. Her heart began to beat fast as his presence rose all around her. Her body slowly relaxed. The connection made, a calming sensation took over her soul.

Then, a vision. *You're in great danger. But Chase will find you. The evil one will not prevail.*

"Great spiritual leader, how will he find me?"

"*He has great powers. Think positive thoughts to guide him to you.*"

The presence disappeared, sending Harmony flying backward. Her sense of renewal and faith soared.

Dusting herself off, she promised herself to think positive. The spiritual mentor knew.

A faint smile curled her mouth. "Yes...Chase will find me."

She leaned against the dirt wall, scared but strong. Her faith in Chase would keep her from doubt. The Creator would guide and keep her safe.

Harmony whispered, "*Keep Chase focused once he learns of my disappearance. Guide him to me.*"

Harmony's heart pusled. "*Could this man be doing this so Chase would sense her being in danger and stop his ceremony early? If this was so, then it will haunt Chase for the rest of his life. He was the only one who could stop this beast.*

Clicking the flashlight off, she closed her eyes, escaping the ear of the situation even if just for a moment; sleep claimed her.

90

Chapter 15

Chase woke under the stars. He realized this was good medicine. Eyes wide from the darkness of the night, he searched for the constellations his mother and grandfather had taught him about gazing at the sky had occupied his mind while growing up without his father. The constellations soothed the mind and body. From a spiritual point, he felt his father among the many constellations.

Images of Harmony raced throughout his mind and the soothing effect of the stars gave way to fear, encasing his every thought. He wanted to flee. A warning echoed inside him.

"My mind is playing tricks on me. I must focus on the positive energy of this place and on the ceremony. Not dwell on the negative images my mind conjures. "

He tossed and turned, but rest was the best medicine. He closed his eyes, praying for morning to arrive.

$$*****$$

The stars faded as dawn broke over the horizon. The center of the ceremonial staff would arrive on Friday. The staff consisted of eagle feathers and yarn hanging from a stick made out of cedar

"Today is Tuesday. Three more days I must wait, but soon everything will be in unison. Once, I'm in balance with Mother Earth, everything else will come. The only fear I have is for Harmony's safety."

$$*****$$

Chase wandered through the next couple of days, paying almost no attention to the daily activities leading up to the ceremony. Eating seemed useless. Nightmares invaded his sleep. In addition, Harmony's safety was at the forefront. On the third day of the ceremony, his uncle approached him to speak of the upcoming events.

"The big day has arrived. Are you ready, my nephew?"

Unable to look his uncle in the eye, Chase merely glanced at him. "Yes, I'm ready. I do this for my people."

"Is there something bothering you? I feel your head is not clear. It must be for this to work."

Chase glanced down, "I'm worried about Harmony. I sense there is something not right."

Chase accepted the ceremonial staff, climbed onto his horse, and rode, his clan beside him. His ancestors stood beside of him in the spirit world. His uncle would ride with him until they reached his Hogan.

＊＊＊＊＊

Arriving at the Hogan of his uncle Wendsler, the medicine man, Chase approached stopping as the reflection of his uncle appeared in front of him.

"I have the ceremonial staff," he said.

His uncle nodded. "Follow me."

Chase walked into the Hogan, sat on buckskin, and handed the staff to his uncle. An air of calmness surrounded them as another medicine man sang a receiving song and inspected the staff.

"Come, it's time to eat," Wendsler announced.

Chase followed his uncle. Hunger played a role in the ceremony, but his stomach churned at the thought of food—or was his thoughts of Harmony's wellbeing causing the inner turmoil?

As evening approached, his uncle chanted the Enemy Way songs. A young girl, dressed in traditional clothing, which consisted of a red dress with beads dangling down the side and buckskin moccasins, skirted across the dirt, dancing to the beat of the drum.

"Drums clear the mind."

The star–filled sky soothed his mind. Chase relinquished his inner spirit to the beat of the drum, momentarily, forgetting his sour stomach. Cleansing and tranquility returned to his soul. He could now walk in beauty and restore harmony among his people.

The wind caressed his face as he lay on the blanket. Anything was possible now.

"Everything will be as it should. I am strong now and can conquer the evil on sacred ground."

Doubt crept into his heart. Why would he doubt? Evil must not win, and he vowed to do everything in his power to make it so.

"Why do I feel so scared? What has occurred that will take my heart and rip it from its entire being?"

Silence filled the empty space. Thoughts of his father flowed in his mind, which triggered his inner soul. Chase spoke to his father for he knew he could hear him in the spirit world.

"Father, you visit me often. What have you come to tell me now?"

Anxiety boiled to the top of his throat. A vivid image of his father formed in his mind. "What do you wish to tell me?"

Flustered, Chase walked into the solitude of his surroundings. He must become one with the Creator.

He followed the image of his father wading out into the creek. The water flowed through the many angles of the creek. Chase sat, offering sage to the spirits.

"Please, spirits, accept what I have offered. I come in a good way. Chaos lives among my people. Please deliver me from ignorance and guide me in the direction in which I should explore and stop the senseless murders."

Chase stood. Time was the only enemy, and he realized his only course of action would be to stop the evil, so tranquility could return to his people.

Chase sprinkled the sage along the water as a turtle emerged.

"Oh, hello there, my friend. I'm sure you're doing your best, my creature friend."

The turtle's slow climb from the water made Chase realize things might arrive in a slow time frame, but they always revealed themselves when the time was right.

"Yes, in time the reservation will return to normal, but the memory will remain forever. Only death reeks on the reservation, and the stain that it has stamped onto the hearts of the people will never tarnish." His father's words echoed through his head.

Chase felt a sense of panic, but realized he was in a dream state. In the vision way. Time was of the essence and he felt a panic seize his insides. He'd been taught by his mother that if dread is felt, then something was about to happen. He tried to linger in the spirit world to see his father and learn what he was trying to tell him, but every time he got close to his image, he would disappear. Chase's leg muscles tightened. Knees locked. Adrenaline spiked. He felt a sense of fleeing.

Thoughts of escape consumed him. *Where to run?*

Chase opened his eyes. Raspy breaths squeezed out of his lungs. With a clenched jaw, he started to dart, but caught himself in time: he was with his people doing the Enemy Way ceremony. *What had just occurred?*

Chase shot glances at his uncle. *What does he know? I need to figure him out.*

"Chase, what's on your mind?"

With tensed arms and hesitant steps, Chase walked toward his uncle.

"I just wonder what you know about my father's death and why you have kept it from me. I know there's something."

Wendsler stepped back, lowering his brow. "Son, in time everything will make sense. This is not the place to discuss the matter."

Muscles jumped in Chase's neck. "I'll find out soon, Uncle, so prepare." Time would reveal what his Uncle was hiding. Thoughts of the secrets etched his mind with doubt. *What could it be and whom would it hurt?*

He shoved his fists inside his pockets. Only time would reveal all the secrets that kept him from understanding why his father died. Would it ever really satisfy him knowing the truth? He missed his father and the father son connection was eliminated upon his death. He loved his father and missed him dearly.

Chase's heart broke and a piece of him was missing due to his father not being with him. *"I will find out what happened and why, then I will take it upon myself to make sure justice is served."*

95

Chapter 16

Dirt crumbled around her. Harmony focused in the dim glow of the flashlight. *The batteries will die soon. How many days have passed?*

Grasping strings of her hair, she screamed, "Let me out of here!" Her voice ricocheted off the walls. Resigned to her predicament, she cradled herself into a corner and slid down the walls, as gravel and dirt pummeled her skin.

"Chase, I need you."

Noise from the opening startled her. She braced herself for the unknown as the makeshift door creaked open and a stocky figure dressed in black with an animal skin masking his face, climbed down into the earth. The figure faced her. "Come."

Harmony pushed herself against the walls as if she could disappear into them. Her eyes clenched shut; the bulky figure approached her, knife blade glinting in the shaft of light from the opening. She gulped. "Leave me alone."

He tightened his scarred hand around her wrist and yanked her to her feet.

"Come."

He pulled her to the ladder, the knife tip to her back. "Climb now or you will regret it."

Cautiously, she obeyed. *I will run when I reach the top.* Her thoughts of escape disappeared as quickly as they'd formed. Another man waited for her as she surfaced and grabbed her by the hair. She answered this attack by scratching and kicking.

The second man threw her to the ground. "We don't want to hurt you, but if you fight, you leave us no choice." The voice was as gruff as his actions.

Fear crept into her heart. These men meant what they said.

"Go," the stocky one said, and shoved her between the shoulders. "We have a long drive."

As she climbed into the beat-up brown truck, she noticed a white feather lying on the ground at her feet. The white feather meant Chase was with her and everything would be all right. Faith. It was what she needed to rely on.

As she leaned against the bed of the truck, her head against the camper shell, the scruffy old man reached back and tied her hands to the makeshift cage in which she had been placed.

"Where are you taking me?"

The old man cinched the ropes tighter.

"You will pay with your lives when Chase comes for me."

The two chuckled and climbed into the truck. As the motor fired up, Harmony's emotions surfaced. Crying uncontrollable, she prayed to the Great Spirit to lead her to a calm place deep inside her.

Sniffling, she tried to free herself. Useless. Laying her head on the carpeted flooring of the makeshift prison in the back of the truck, she closed her eyes.

Please, Chase. Come soon.

Lost in fear and grief, she closed her eyes and prayed.

✶ ✶ ✶ ✶ ✶

The whoosh of passing cars roused her. She peeked out the small, dusty camper window. Red mountains loomed in the distance. Stiff and achy from hours on the road, she wondered how far they'd come and where they were.

"Was this the Navajo reservation? Why have they brought me here?" She wondered.

The truck came to a halt. Her heart raced. *Now what?*

Opening the back, the two men forced her out, feet first.

"Where are we?"

They grabbed her arms.

"You're hurting me!"

"Shut up."

"I demand to know where we are!" She cried.

"Navajo land," the smaller man spit out.

The bulky guy smacked him. "Don't give her any information."

"Don't smack me."

"Boss gave specific instructions. We are to say nothing. Just transport her."

Harmony flinched. "Who is your boss? Tell him to face me."

He chuckled. "You'll meet him soon, and your boyfriend will die."

Bile rose to her throat. "Chase is better than any of you! Wait and see who's going die."

"This way. Stand still while I untie your hands."

The skinny man with a scar led her down a rocky path that wound through the desert for miles. After what seemed like hours, they stopped abruptly.

"The cave is over here."

Harmony kicked at the unpleasant man. "You cannot put me in a cave."

"It's two against one. You have no choice," he smirked.

She pushed against the skinny, lanky man with the scar on his right cheek, and he lost his footing and grabbed for a branch from a nearby shrub. With one hefty kick, she scrambled free. She ran down an embankment. Her feet slid on the loose rock and failed to hold her footing. Legs sprawled, she rolled to the bottom. Rocks and dirt pelted her skin.

Coming to a halt at the bottom of the ravine, she moaned.

"Go get her," the older one ordered.

The younger, skinny man with the scar grabbed her arm. "Where'd you think you're going?"

He led her around some brush and to a dark cave deep inside of Navajo Land. As they entered the cave, the cold and dark enveloped her.

"How do you expect to keep me in here?" she challenged.

As if on cue, both men chuckled, rounded a corner and came face to face with a cage large enough for one human, that hung from the ceiling, dangling as if food for an animal. Just big enough for her. Flashlights, water, and food were piled inside. They meant to keep her alive. For now.

They shoved her through the small opening and locked the doors.

Tears welled in her eyes. "Please don't do this."

"You have what you need."

Her heart sank as the two ruthless men walked away, leaving her in a place where she could sense evil. She glanced around the cave. Malevolence lurked in the cave, the darkness amplifying its presence.

She slumped to the floor of her cage. "Chase, please come soon."

The words echoed in the dark chamber. Tears rolled down her cheeks. She must have faith. Chase would save her and the wicked men would pay.

The echo of footsteps faded. Silence pressed against her ears. Her chin trembled, her stomach ached, and her heart thudded dully in her chest. But how would he ever find her?

Chapter 17

Chase's heart pulsated. "Harmony." Fear for her safety flooded his mind.

Stranded in the middle of nowhere, he was helpless. Wringing his hands, he stepped outside into the morning mist.

A commotion outside drew his attention. Fellow officer Hooke waved and motioned for him to come to his patrol unit.

"Chase, I came as soon as we knew for sure. I'm sorry, man, but this is going to ruin your ceremony."

"What are you trying to tell me?'

"It's Harmony. She's missing."

A lump swelled inside his throat. "What the hell are you talking about?"

"Nobody's heard from or seen her in days."

Chase felt the blood drain from his face, unable to move, and the inability to speak forced him to his knees. *Harmony is in danger. I must go and find her.*

Officer Hook dashed to his side. "Chase, man, are you okay?'

Clenching his jaw, he pushed him away. "I have to handle this my way."

Chase rose and walked to his Hogan. He gathered his belongings and dumped them into a sack.

"Chase, what's going on?" His Uncle had appeared beside him.

His nostrils flared. "Harmony's missing, Uncle Wendsler. I must leave."

"Son, you have to finish the ceremony."

He narrowed his eyes. "You can't stop me. The one person that means the most to me is in danger and I'm leaving now."

He swiped his uncle's arm back as he pushed his way past him.

"Chase, wait!"

He pivoted to his uncle. "What is it?"

"Take this arrowhead. It will protect you from evil."

"Thank you, Uncle." Placing the arrowhead in his pocket, he nodded at Officer Hooke. He climbed into his truck and headed back into town.

His entire soul pondered the unthinkable. *Who would do this, and why? Is Harmony still alive?*

Thoughts of escape clouded his mind. He grabbed the steering wheel tightly as he pulled into his driveway where'd he last seen Harmony. The circular drive with burden baskets lined the porch. *She was standing right there.* The image of her shadowed in his mind. *Harmony loved the burden baskets. How can I deal with it if I lose her?* Clasping his medicine bundle tightly, he prayed that he could overcome the fear inside his heart. He counted four patrol units parked at random.

He climbed out of the vehicle, his jaw fiercely set, flushed with an intense, adrenaline spike.

"There are signs, spirits. Show me."

Blowing caution to the wind, he entered the house. Nostrils flaring, he fast walked past the officers and down the hall leading to their bedroom.

"Harmony," he said, his voice a guttural roar. "Where are you?"

*****

Darkness consumed her. The cage enraged her. She wasn't an animal but yet she felt like one.

"I must be strong. Chase will find me soon."

Beating the metal wire feverishly with her hands brought some emotional relief, but left her hands bruised and sore. "Let me out of here!"

A sound, like claws scratched the wall, grabbed her attention. She cocked her head and slowly, her eyes drifted to the floor. Glowing eyes stared at her. A coyote's eyes. Its gray coat sparkled as it lurked around the cage that dangled in the air. *Does he think I was his dinner?* The glaring eyes stared. His vicious teeth

102

gritted together, revealing his strength.

Focus, Harmony. Don't show fear to this animal. He's a trickster. Chase warned me about this jokester. Beware of the dark side of things looming about.

Harmony refocused. Her thoughts went to Chase.

"My instincts are good. Chase will find me. Or am I deceiving myself?" Weariness overtook her, leaving the scent of this damp, dark place ingrained in her mind, and the residue a sticky reminder in her mouth.

"He will come." She swallowed. "Soon."

$$\star\star\star\star\star$$

Combing outside in search of clues, he felt her presence. "Show me, Harmony."

A loud screech echoed throughout the canyon. He searched the skies for the answer he feared would not come. But there it was! The hawk!

The bird of prey swooped low, revealing the importance of timing.

"Guide me, sacred one. What are you trying to reveal?"

Chase turned to the chattering close by. Harmony's adopted family had arrived and was offering protection prayers to the spirits. Pain seized him. Thoughts of harm coming to her overwhelmed him.

His stomach rolled as he approached, dreading the inevitable. "I will find Harmony. I'll protect her with my life."

"What if it is too late?" Harmony's godmother swallowed.

Chase's hand rested on Harmony's godmother and he embraced her with strength.

"I know you will try Chase. Why has this happened? What can you tell me? Does the killer have her?"

Chase hesitated. "I can't be for certain." He swallowed hard. "But it could be." "Why would anyone want to harm my god daughter? Tears streaked down her mother's face.

"I will bring her home safe....I promise."

Cradling his arm around Harmony's godmother, Chase's determination to keep his promise doubled. He would not let her down. Harmony became her god daughter during her Sunrise Ceremony.

$$\ast\,\ast\,\ast\,\ast\,\ast$$

Waiting for a sign to show him which road to follow, Chase paced the short distance across the porch. Then, there... Under the doormat... Owl feathers. The sign was obvious, the warning severe: Harmony's life was in great danger.

Chase scooped the owl feathers into his hands. A visit with Ralan would be necessary. Heat coursed through his veins.

I'm coming Ralan, for I know you have her. You will beg to tell me where she is, once I'm done with you.

His voice choked with tears, he continued, *I will die before I let anything happen to Harmony. She's my life and I won't lose her again.*

The overpowering fear he had to face captured his spirit, while the regret of leaving her alone smothered his every ounce of inner turmoil. But he would use his last breath to save her.

Chapter 18

Ralan leaned back on the wooden door to the entrance to his vet office. He glanced around, taking in the sparse vegetation of the reservation. A tumbleweed skirted across the dry, barren land. His one-roomed cluttered office served the residents well treating the animals the brought in, so he had seen no need to upgrade to a bigger place.

A photograph of his mother hung on the wall. Brushing his hand across her cheek as if to wipe a tear from her face made him feel her closeness.

"Hello, Ralan," a deep voice echoed.

Pivoting on his heels, Ralan turned slowly.

Piercing eyes locked on Officer Spirit Walker. "What are you doing here?"

"Harmony Wind Dancer is missing. What can you tell me about that?"

A crooked smile emerged. "Well, it sounds like she stuck her pretty little nose where it doesn't belong."

Chase punched Ralan in the left cheek and he fell to the floor.. "If anything happens to her, I swear you'll pay. You disrespect our people. They need to know the real you."

He brushed the dust from his clothes. "I should file charges against you but you're the law around here and nobody would believe me over you."

Kicking the door open, Chase's boots clanked against the wood. The look of death spread over his face as he climbed into his patrol unit.

Quick on his heels, Ralan followed him to the door. "You better stay off my property and leave me the hell alone!" he hollered.

"I will be back." The engine roared and he slammed the truck into drive. The tires spun. Dust pelted the area.

Ralan slammed the door. "Officer-know-it-all will pay for coming onto my land and humiliating me this way. His precious Harmony deserves what she gets."

*****

The morning sun crested the horizon. Chase sipped his coffee, looking out of the bay window, wondering what his next move should be. *Follow Ralan? Or scout on his own?*

"I must speak to Uncle Wendsler."

He packed his gear and headed out the door. He slid his bag into the seat and reached for his phone.

"Police Department, how can I help you?"

"Lori, it's Chase. Is the Chief in?"

"No, Chase, he isn't," the dispatcher said. "Can I take a message?"

"Tell him I'm heading to the Navajo Reservation. I feel my uncle can help us find Harmony. If anything happens, let Officer Hooke handle it. I'll be back in a couple of days. Let Chief know that I found out Ralan's vet business has grown. He has an office on the Navajo Reservation."

"I'll let him know as soon as he comes in. Also, it's been a week since the last murder. Hopefully they will stop."

"Thank you, Lori. Yes, I hope we've seen the last of the murders."

He tossed the phone into the seat, his prayers going to Harmony. "Great Spirit, protect her from harm. She helps others and comes in a good way."

Chase felt her near his soul. His only concern was for her safe return, but his heart remained heavy. If she were harmed, he would never forgive himself.

*****

Full of potholes, the winding, dusty road jarred his thoughts. As the old farmhouse came into view, memories of his dad grew vivid.

The tall cactus stood erect giving way to the morning sun. The dust forced his brakes to squeal. He shifted into park; Chase

106

glanced up and saw his uncle standing on the porch.

He stepped out of the truck, nodded toward his uncle.

"Any news of Harmony?"

"No, Uncle. She's still missing. No new clues. I don't know where to look or who to ask. Everything's a blur. You must help me. I have the impression you know something."

Wendsler cupped Chase's elbow. "Come, we need to talk. I've been waiting."

They climbed the hill, silence prevailing.

Then Wendsler spoke. "Chase, I believe the reservation murders are tied to the murder of your father. There have been similar crimes, but nobody's has done anything about it. I've been investigating, and the murders on both reservations are similar in nature to your father's. The other thing I find interesting is that beads were also left at the scene of your father's murder."

Chase gaped at him. "What? I wasn't told of this. What the hell is going on?"

"Stay calm. Harmony's life is on the line."

"I thought Ralan had something to do with the murders. How is all this related?"

"I believe Ralan's connected in some way. I've kept my eyes on him when he's on the Navajo Land. He's been hanging with some awful dudes. He's turned to the dark side....shapeshifter."

"What would cause him to take Harmony? She has nothing to do with this."

"They want you, and what better way to lure you in? They feel you have a connection to something they want. Ralan's involved with this, but I can't yet tell how."

Chase kicked the rocks under his feet, pondering what the link could be, when a snorting sound came from behind a big clump of bushes.

He pulled his gun and stared in the direction of the noise. The nickering gave way to the most beautiful horse, tan in color with black legs and mane.

As the horse turned toward Chase, he understood. On the horse's forehead, right above his eyes, a black circular spot in the form of a dream catcher was etched into the many different colors of his hair.

"Uncle, look. A dream catcher," Chase said, pointing to the horse's head.

"This is a sign for us to take note. This horse knows. I've never seen him around here before."

Chase moved closer to the noble animal. "You are unique. What have you come to tell me?"

With a wide grin, Chase reached out to pet the remarkable spirit that stood before him, his heart beating in his throat as he placed his hand on the sacred animal.

He shook his head, losing his train of thought.

"Uncle, this horse is special. His dark brown eyes make me think of Dad."

"He appears to know something, all right." Wendsler agreed.

Dusk settled on the ranch as vivid colors streaked the sacred land.

Chase stood in silence, waiting to see the horse offer his friendship. As darkness shadowed its features, the horse nudged Chase's face.

"You're special. I'll name you Dream Catcher. Please show me the signs."

Chase led the horse to his uncle's barn.

"I will stay in the barn with Dream Catcher tonight. Tomorrow he'll show me what to do."

Chase closed the barn door. He bit his lower lip, wondering if turmoil would rise with the dawning sun.

Chapter 19

Raffish chuckling woke Harmony. She squinted from the darkness of the cave, but managed to see her captors standing in a circle talking and conjuring a plan.

"Ralan....oh my God...he's involved....."

Harmony strained to hear. Ralan glanced toward her. She closed her eyes, pretending she was asleep, but watching his every move out of the corner of her eye.

The clacking of Ralan's steel-toed boots increased her uneasiness. She felt his presence and focused on remaining still.

His labored breathing forced her to open her eyes.

"Well, you;re awake."

Harmony pushed away from the metal cage. "You are evil Ralan. Why are you doing this? You hurt your own father."

"You will find out soon enough."

He walked away snickering, forced her words. "Chase will come for me. You'll regret everything you have done."

Ralan sighed, and then stopped in his footsteps, "He'll die. It's his destiny."

Harmony flinched and screamed. "You'll be the one to die."

Ralan faded into the shadows along with his sickening laugh.

"So, that's the reason they took me. They only want Chase."

Harmony held her stomach as she clenched her teeth together. The churning inside her wouldn't stop. The pain increased, sending a torrent of vomit onto her lap.

*****

Chase woke with the rising sun. Dream Catcher stood over him, pawing with his front feet.

"What is it, boy? You seem to be excited. What do you know?"

In a flash, the horse darted out of the barn, Chase hot on his heels. Tail tucked with upper brow furrowed, Dream Catcher raced around in circles in the front yard.

"Come, boy, what's wrong? Show me."

Dream Catcher reared, forcing Chase to grab the reins of Spirit, his uncle's horse, and climbed on.

The terrain turned rocky. Pebbles skidded down the mountainside. Dream Catcher kept his distance but never left Chase to far behind. He knew something.

Dream Catcher stopped abruptly, striking his front legs against the dirt. Chase jumped off Spirit, and ran to the nearby rocks. He peeked through, and slumped backward.

Ralan leaned against his truck. Hoodlums chuckled, taking in his every word.

Chase strained to hear the conversation.

"Okay, guys, you've done a good job. It won't be long and it will all be over. Once, I get my hands on the ancient beaded amulets that hold the hawk and wolf, my powers will be the strongest."

Puzzled, Chase held his breath, *"Ancient beaded amulet of the hawk and wolf."*

The conversation continued.

"Yeah, the ancient amulet, which is in the form of a dream catcher, holds great powers from our medicine men of long ago. Once in my possession, I will be unstoppable."

Chase edged away from the rocks. He must speak to his uncle. Darkness lurked on the reservation, which only meant one thing: Harmony's safety was in jeopardy, and she was his prime objective.

＊＊＊＊＊

"Come on, Spirit, we must ride hard. Dream Catcher, come on, boy." The ride seemed to go on forever when Chase finally spotted his Uncle's house just ahead.

Dust filtered through the air, as Chase loomed to a stop. He jumped off the horse, screaming, "Uncle, we must speak! Ralan's here and I heard him mention an amulet, one with special powers."

"Shhh...Chase, I know of this amulet. It's said to contain the highest of powers for a medicine man. Whoever owns it will be granted these powers, and it can be used for good or evil."

"We must find it before Ralan does."

"Chase, the amulet is the most sacred of all. Some even fear it. Your father died protecting it."

"What! You knew this and never told me, even when the murders started occurring? Hell, on the radio it said another murder took place last night, here on the Navajo reservation, as you sit by and do nothing."

"Don't speak to me that way. Your father taught you to respect your elders."

"My father, you want to speak his name. Don't bring him into this. Where is the amulet?"

"It's in a safe place, until it's needed. Your father gave it to me the day he died. It's yours once you become a medicine man, but it can be used in emergency situations."

"The amulet holds the key to the murders and to Harmony. Give it to me! I must get Harmony back safely."

"No, you can't trade the power of the amulet for Harmony. Ralan's trying to coax you into doing just that. He realizes you're the keeper of the amulet. The power within it should only be used for good, not his wicked ways. To break the tradition would only cause death on the reservations....forever."

Chase gritted his teeth as he paced the room.

"What am I to do, Uncle? I have to stop the murders, but I also have to protect Harmony. If I give in to Ralan, then his darkness will take over the reservations and our people. Yet to keep it could mean Harmony's death."

"Let's have some coffee and talk. There's a way, but dangerous to all of us. The amulet must remain in our possession, or destruction will remain and there will be a lot more deaths."

He patted Chase on the back, and followed him inside.

*****

Harmony's mind wandered. Drained from her emotions, she sipped on the water.

Where is Chase? Wonder how Joe is doing?

Her muscles ached and twitched due to the cramped cage. Light filtered in and voices echoed through the cave walls.

Harmony strained to hear the whispers.

"Chase Spirit Walker's arrived. I saw him at his uncle's house. Soon we will have the power."

The dainty man with rimmed glasses chuckled.

"We must rid the world of that good *ye enaaldlooshii,* shapeshifter. He shall fail and we shall win."

"Hold on, Sam. Chase is very powerful. We must get the amulet first, and then take care of him. My powers will then be greater than his, and nobody can stop me."

"So, what's for tonight? Must we kill again? Ralan, I've lost count of how many we've already sacrificed. Don't we have to kill a certain number of medicine men before we touch the amulet?"

Ralan cocked his head, drummed his feet into the dirt floor.

"What do you mean you've lost count? You ditz! You best get to remembering, or you're no good to me. At least one hundred must go. Between the two reservations, the count rose to ninety-eight, so we have two more before we can get the amulet. Are you burying most of the bodies so that tribal cop doesn't find them?"

Sam scowled. "Tonight death shall return. Who are we aiming for? Yes, boss, we have buried most of the bodies in different desolate places on both reservations."

Ralan turned to face his followers, a gleam in his eye. He glanced around summing up his men. Some seem timid, while others were ready to start an all-out war. Ralan knew Chase would call them hoodlums. Most of them wore tattoos, piercings, and rarely took a shower.

"Tonight we must aim for another medicine man. I think we shall scout tonight and find one who is practicing at the time we choose to end his life."

Chuckling ricocheted off the walls, vibrating across the sound barrier.

Harmony cringed.

Chase, please hurry, She prayed. *More lives will be lost tonight. Our medicine men are dying. But where are all the bodies hidden of our medicine men?*

Harmony closed her eyes and transferred herself to a peaceful spot where only good subsided.

Please, Creator, guide Chase and protect our people from the evil surrounding us. Please let Joe be okay, for he is a good man.

Sleep connected to her soul, where peace knew her name.

Chapter 20

Thinking became his nightmare. Chase paced.

"Uncle, we know shapeshifters are hard to kill. They wreak havoc on our people. Their eyes are pure heinous, glowing red like the owl. They have the power to read our thoughts. So, how are we supposed to kill them?"

"Chase, their powers are strong and dangerous. When this goes down, we must cover ourselves with corn pollen for protection. Now we know Ralan is a shapeshifter, we have the power to kill him."

"Why he decided to go this way, I'll never understand. He must have the Ghost sickness, because he's consumed with the death of his mother."

"Ralan practices the Witchery Way. He's an *'ant'jjhnii,* witch. I wonder if he didn't kill his mother himself."

Chase paused. "Uncle, it makes sense! Judi had been sick for several months before she fell off that horse. I bet he used *'iinzhjjd,* the evil–wishing magic. He had opportunities to gather her hair, or some of her personal items, to perform this. It would cause a slow death."

"Now you're seeing the big picture. Ralan is vengeful. He must be stopped, but you can't allow personal feelings to get in the way."

Chase pulled at his ear. "I must protect our people," he said, anger exploding on his face.

"Uncle, I know Joe is Apache but do you know if Judi was also?"

"Judi was Navajo." Chase stated.

Silence ensued.

"Chase, we need to perform the Protection Ceremony so you are shielded from the dark wrath. We also should do a ceremony to bring out the shapeshifters."

Feeling trapped, Chase leaned against the wall. "I'm unsure of many things, Uncle. How do I pick between our people and the only woman I love?"

Hands behind his head, Wendsler leaned back. "Son, you will figure it out. I know your heart. Believe in yourself, it will guide you in the right direction."

Chase tightened his fists. "You're right, Uncle. I can do this. The Creator gave me the power. I am a shapeshifter. I'm the hawk, powerful."

His Uncle thrust a fist toward the sky. "I knew you would overcome. You are your father's son."

Chase reached for his uncle, embracing him as a warrior.

"Thank you, Uncle. I now see what must be done. You've been a great teacher. I'm sorry for ever doubting you about my father. You were only trying to protect me."

$$*\;*\;*\;*\;*$$

Dampness soaked her bones. Emptiness invaded her heart. Vile brewed in the cold, darkness of the cave.

"Come, let me explain tonight's rules."

Ralan's laughter sent cold chills up Harmony's spine.

She cradled herself, humming to drown the cold chuckle and rocked back and forth.

Chase's powers outweigh Ralan's, good over evil.

Her heart held doubt, but she kept her faith.

The voices grew louder. She went quiet and closed her eyes in an attempt to hear the strains of conversation between her and her captives.

"Sam, tonight we kill another medicine man. Do you have everything ready?"

"Oh, yes, sir. All your charms are in your bag."
"Good. The amulet is our strongest need. Once in our possession only, evil will remain. Tonight everyone must follow my lead. Do all of you understand?"

"Yes, boss, we got it," came the echoes.

Ralan grabbed the back of her head and filled it with her soft hair through the cage, forcing her face against the steel bars. She screamed.

"Harmony, this will all be over soon. You will die a slow death with your darling Chase. You put your nose where it didn't belong. You know too much, unless of course you want to join our side."

She spit at him, the glob landing on his cheek. "Never. Evil doesn't know my name. You will be the loser."

He forced her face against the cage. "You will die and will regret not joining forces with me."

Harmony jutted her chin. "I'll have the satisfaction to watch as you crumble. You will be your own demise!"

Ralan glowered. "You will be the one to watch as Chase is consumed by the wrath we will bestow on him. Watching the life drain out of him will be the only satisfaction I need."

Harmony watched the blemished face of her captor as the boasting men careened through the tunnel.

Her shoulders slumped. When would this nightmare end?

"Creator, find peace within our souls to help us get closure. Hinder the evil, let the good prevail."

She let her mind flutter into a world all her own, where peace comforted the soul.

*****

Chase prepared for the smudging ceremony. Bracing for the onslaught of evil would take a while. Each medicine would serve a purpose. Sage, tobacco, sweet grass, and cedar were all used for calling of the spirits.

"Uncle, the four medicines will guide us. Sage helps to cleanse us, tobacco helps speak to the spirits, sweet grass is the sacred hair to Mother Earth, which brings good spirits to us, and cedar is used to purify our bodies."

"Yes, these medicines will guide us. Tonight we will mix the tobacco and cedar together to call out to our spirits for direction."

Chase felt glad that he had at last mended his relationship with his father's brother. Having Wendsler on his side gave him a renewed sense of purpose, as though his father were speaking to him through his Uncle.

Night wrapped its arms around Mother Earth. Crickets serenaded the forest and all its creatures. The smudging ceremony would release all the good spirits and make everything pure.

Chase edged his way out of the creaky front door to welcome the dusk of night. Soon shapeshifters would emerge. The illusion of the night sky evoked mysteries of their own.

"Chase, over here."

Chase glanced. "Uncle, what a beautiful site for the smudging ceremony."

The circle made out of rocks heightened the monumental walls of red mountains. Inside the circle, the sacred medicines waited.

"Come, we must get this started."

Chase stepped into the circle.

"Stand still as I pass these sacred medicines over your body for protection. Also, say your prayer to the Creator and your spirit guides."

Chase nodded an understanding, and the ceremony began.

The sacred medicines misted his body as his prayer evoked the spirits. "Creator, I ask for guidance and a clear mind. Evil ravages our home. Please keep Harmony safe until I can rescue her. Let the power of goodness prevail. The amulet and its power shall remain with me. Thank you, and please light my way."

Chase's uncle infused him with sage, sweet grass, tobacco, and cedar.

Once the cleansing swept over Chase's body, he took the remaining cedar and tobacco and sprinkled over the embers into the burning fire. The smoke from the medicines drew the attention of the spirits.

Clasping the sacred amulet, which hung from his neck, he offered another prayer, "Please accept my offerings. I come in a good way, offering you my inner strength. Guide me into the light of goodness."

He raised his arms toward the sky, releasing his fear.

Chase sighed, closed his eyes and stood in the circle for hours. Honoring his people, he felt a renewed calm.

Sensing eyes watching, he swerved around on his heels. But all was darkness. "I am prepared. Come and fight when you are ready!" he spoke aloud.

The crackling of twigs lingered as footsteps carried the watcher away.

"Soon, Harmony, hold on. Everything will be okay."

Chase perceived that the ones watching him would let Ralan know what he was doing. He would face this man head on to protect his woman and his people. His faced flushed as the blood raced to his face.

What made the entirely thing worst was that they were toying with the life he had planned for Harmony. He would stop this murderer. He placed his faith into the Creator. This was the only way.

Chapter 21

Sam sprinted into the cave. "Ralan, I just saw Chase perform the smudging ceremony. He's preparing for the battle."

Ralan's face revealed disgust. "I expected him to prepare. He's a smart man; but he doesn't understand the power he is up against. It appears you doubt me also."

"It's not that, but are you prepared for the potency of his battle?"

Ralan loomed over Sam. "What the hell are you talking about? I'm stronger than any shapeshifter, especially him. Never forget that!" He pushed Sam against the wall, as he stomped his way past him.

Ralan crossed his arms and stood in a wide stance. Adrenaline rushed through his body at the mere thought of taking away Chase's power.

"I'm the most powerful shapeshifter. Watch as I crumble that good shapeshifter, taking his powers. Then the amulet belongs to me."

Sam bowed his head. "Sorry for making it sound as if you aren't ready. Soon, you will rise to power and show all these weaklings who is in charge."

Ralan grunted. "Yes, I will rule the entire reservations. I am Navajo and Apache. I shall reveal the power that boils in my blood."

Sam stood erect. "We will rule."

"Correct, my friend; now let's go get that medicine man."

They stalked out of the cave. A medicine man with great power would die at the hands of a mad man.

*****

Coyotes howled in the distance, the warmth of the night encircling Mother Earth. Death would arrive soon.

Ralan, Sam, and the members of his team prowled through the barren land in search of a victim.

The unearthly cries from the coyote or trickster urged the killing. Ralan dressed in his coyote pelt as Sam covered himself with the bear.

Red, piercing eyes beamed through the darkness.

As predicted, the powerful medicine man was working tensely, practicing the chants that had been handed down to him from his ancestors. John Little Horse lived on the Navajo reservation in unity with all living things. He was the ideal victim for Ralan.

Mutely moving, they were on their victim.

"Sam, hand me the bone beads," Ralan whispered.

Placing the beads into a blowgun, then releasing them set his blood to pumping.

The beads pelted the victim. The medicine man grabbed his side and slumped to the ground. Breathless. His life floated around him. The spirit world welcomed him. Bone beads trapped his body.

Ralan sat thrilled. "Get ready. Once he collapses to the ground we go in."

The medicine man's body crumbled to the dirt. Making their move quickly, Ralan darted toward the lifeless body, with extreme swiftness. He loomed over the victim. "You have great power, and I need it."

He clawed the man with his sharp, razor nails to reveal his power. Blood spilled to the ground. The lifeless body lay before them, eyes open and the soul released into the spirit world. Ralan's smirk revealed his true sinister nature beneath the coyote's mask.

Swiftly turning, the shapeshifters disappeared into the night leaving the mark of death once again.

✶✶✶✶✶

Blood infused their clothing.

"Sam, now all we have to do is find one more medicine man."

Sam removed the stained clothing. "Yeah, but who and where are we going to find that person?"

Ralan eased against the cold walls of the cave.

"Oh, but the best is saved for the last. Our next kill will be... Wendsler Spirt Walker, Chase's uncle."

Harmony's heart skipped a beat. "No, leave him alone!"

Ralan turned to the prickly voice. "You can't do anything about it. Officer Know-It-All will have no choice but to hand over the amulet for his uncle's life. Once in my possession, they both die anyway."

"How do you know Chase has this amulet?" Harmony growled.

Chuckling, Ralan responded, "The power of the shapeshifter informed me to who holds it."

"Chasc will never give in to you. He doesn't work that way. He travels the good red road and will never step a foot on the black road."

"Let's make a bet. If I break Chase, you will become my woman of darkness. Deal?"

Harmony felt nauseated. "Never!"

"Wait and see. You have no choice, and by the way, John Little Horse gave us more energy tonight."

As Ralan stalked his way back to the entrance of the cave, Harmony watched as he disappeared and turned her head to pray.

"Please, hear my plea, Creator. Another person died tonight at the hands of evil. Please help their families to cope with their premature death. Protect Chase and his uncle. They come with a good heart."

Bitlng her upper lip, she felt helpless, against the darkness that dwelled. Then her heart leaped with pride: Chase will win, she thought. Faith entered her soul and she would keep it tucked there with positive thoughts.

Ralan turned to darkness. Why? Only his spirit knew the answer. Now that he has so much blood on his hands, his ancestors would be disappointed.

She fumbled for words. "Creator, *Usen*, protect the good way and rip the evil from our lives. There are shapeshifters who use their power for their own sick ways. The good shapeshifters use their power to help protect our people. Give us all strength to overcome such hideous crimes against our fellow man. Amen."

Chapter 22

Chase briskly bolted to the murder scene.

"Officer Begaye, what've you learned? Were there beads left at the scene?"

"Same ammo, swift kill, and yes, beads were left by the victim's body."

Scratching his head, Chase turned to his uncle. "You need to check on Joe. If he's awake, he might be able to tell us something more about his son. I need to stay here and learn what I can about the evil at work.

Wendsler patted Chase on the back. "I'll run off into the sunset and go check on our friend; I should be back by dinner."

"Thanks. Please travel with caution."

He turned to Officer Begaye. "How can I help? I know this is out of my jurisdiction but the same type of murders is occurring on my reservation, and they all have the same ammo. Ralan Spirit Eyes is our prime suspect."

"We can use all the help we can get. There have been random murders for the past six months, where the killer leaves the beads, and all of them have been medicine men."

"Okay, the body is stiff, so it's been here for a while. Let me get a closer look at how it's positioned. He's laying face-down, which indicates he was struck from behind." Kneeling down, Chase focused. "Look, bone beads embedded into his back. Once the victim's down, the killer approaches and kills quickly."

Officer Begay squatted. "Yeah, I see that now. So, the killer strikes with bone beads, then comes in for the kill once the victim is nearly unconscious. It also appears they are aiming at medicine men. This will be our fourth one."

"So, this one is local"?"

"Yeah, they all were except one. This medicine man has practiced for a long time around these parts. He performed my daughters *Kinaalda*, the coming of age ceremony to adulthood."

Officer Begaye grabbed his camera. "Snapping pictures of the scene is our next step. Then we'll remove the body."

"Okay, bro; let me know if you come up with anything else. I'll be at my uncle's house."

Chase jumped into the pickup and wiped the sweat off his brow. *What are they doing, targeting medicine men? Research on this amulet has to become my focus. I must concentrate. They could kill Harmony. Focus, Chase.*

✶✶✶✶✶

The road to the Valley never changed, miles and miles of cactus and beautiful, endless mountains.

"Well, let me see what I can find on this radio." Wendsler shook his head in frustration. "Hmm, only station that comes through is country. I don't even know music anymore. It's become more of trying to understand the words."

Driving down the freeway to the Phoenix area turned into a time of recapturing his soul.

All at once, the power of the hawk swooped down, crossing his path, and causing him to swerve.

"What are you warning me about?" he wondered.

Wendsler cautiously heeded the warning of something bad or good was on its way, watching with a crooked eye as he traveled on his journey.

He took note of how few exits there were, sighing with irritation, when unexpectedly an older, blue truck with tinted windows and no license plate rammed into his bumper. Wendsler swerved into the other lane, barely missing the oncoming traffic.

The aggressor bumped the back of the truck with greater force.

Scowling, Wendsler pressed the gas pedal. Reaching speeds of more than eighty sent his anger into overdrive. "Man, get off my ass," he growled.

The truck kept on his tail. Inside, it appeared to be a man with dark hair.

The unknown person pulled beside the truck, Wendsler braced himself. The brunt of the two trucks sent Wendsler off the side of the road.

He clasped the steering wheel. "Are you fucking kidding me?" The dirt penetrated the truck, sending rocks through the open window.

Jerking to a complete stop, the hard impact sent Wendsler's upper body into the windshield.

The dust settled, and Wendsler reached for his shotgun, fearing he would have to use it, praying he wouldn't. He scanned the area. The blue truck had vanished.

Relieved, he stepped out his vehicle and examined it. "Not much damage, old horse. I think we can continue on our journey."

Jumping back inside, he turned the switch. Shifting the truck into drive, he hit the gas, sending the truck into a spin.

"Let's go, old horse; we can't let them defeat us."

Wendsler glimpsed in the rearview mirror, taking note of the blood trickling down his forehead.

"Damn it," he said, wiping the blood away.

The rest of the journey was uneventful, giving him time to collect his thoughts.

"Are the evil ones after me now? If so, they'll be after Chase soon."

Thinking of what could be on its way, he felt apprehension mixed with caution. For Wendsler realized the battle would be devastating.

"I must call Chase. He needs to know that he may be next."

✶✶✶✶✶

Chase clicked the keyboard. "Where can I find out about the amulet and its power? It's as if it's a mystery."

The phone rang. "Hello."

Nothing but silence came through the landline until Wendsler's hoarse voice began to speak.

"Chase, it's me, your Uncle. I wanted to let you know I made it to the hospital in one piece."

"Uncle, what do you mean? You sound stressed."

"A blue truck ran me off the road."

Chase went cold. "Are you okay?"

"Yeah, banged up a little, and the truck has some damage."

"Are you sure you're okay? I know we've had out differences but you're my only family now."

"I just wanted to give you a heads up in case they target you next, which I suspect they will."

"Be careful coming home. Have you seen Joe yet?"

"I'm waiting for visiting hours, since he's still in ICU."

"Look out for yourself, Uncle."

"You too, my son. Watch the windows."

The silence on the phone brought Chase back to his surroundings. Darkness crept upon Mother Earth. Chase glanced out the window, pulling down the shade. Shapeshifters aimed to scare. They use bone beads to capture their victims. Time was ticking away, so he returned to his research. Hours passed and Chase yawned and stretched. He stood and walked to the window and peeked out the blinds. Nothing.

Chase resumed his research when the window glass splintered and shattered to the floor. Chase dropped to the ground just in time, as the cursed bone beads flew through the air, penetrating the wall.

He grabbed his gun out of its holster and crawled to the door. He peeked out for movement, scanning the area; nothing. He cracked the door and crawled through the opening on his belly. The shapeshifter disappeared into the darkness without a trace except for the bone beads imbedded in the walls.

Chase leaned against the porch railing. The shapeshifters would not stop until they got what they wanted....the amulet.

Chapter 23

Harmony turned toward the commotion, while biting her dirty fingernails, she waited.

She rocked in place as she prayed, "Creator, protect Chase from evil. He's a good man, stubborn but honorable. He's in grave danger. His heart floods with good deeds. Send our ancestor spirits to guide him, *doleelgo at'ee*, Amen."

Impulsively, her eyes focused toward the entrance to the damp, dark cave.

"How long have I been here?" She whispered her words faintly.

"You've been here for a week," the gruff voice replied from behind the thick walls.

"Why are you helping Ralan?" she asked.

Sam shouted to get her attention. "He's powerful, and once he wrap's you up in his power, you can't let go."

"Yes, you can. You're not alone in this fight. Do the right thing by helping me to escape. We can go to Chase and he will protect you."

"Stop it." Sam retorted, nostrils flaring.

"But you can be a good man if…"

"SHUT UP! You have no idea about my life and the struggles I've experienced. I will gain power from helping Ralan."

"That's what he wants you to believe, but once he's done with you then he will throw you away like you were nothing."

Sam exploded. "I will break every bone in your body, or even better, shoot bone beads into you and laugh as you slowly die!"

Harmony's raspy breaths sent her into quiet mode. She realized she was causing intense emotional responses in Sam; the best thing to do was to remain quiet and not infuriate him any further.

Her heart felt for this man, lost…his inner soul confused. Evil worked that way slowly taking over a soul and causing it to be lost. She prayed silently, hoping he would come to his senses and help her, which in turn would help his in own soul. Yet doubt lingered in her thoughts.

* * * * *

The long corridors leading to Joe's room filled with family members waiting to see their sick loved ones. Wendsler sat in an old blue recliner and waited for visiting hours, which, according to the clock wall, would commence in five minutes.

He'd been flipping idly through a magazine when the nurse announced *visiting hours.*

His worn cowboy boots, sprinkled with dirt, clanked down the hallway. Wendsler hobbled through the double doors, the pain apparent from the confrontation between the two vehicles had caused injury in which he hadn't expected.

With the exception of the occasional beep from the monitors, the room was quiet. His pulse quickened. He pulled up a chair and sat in quiet contemplation next to Joe, when the heart monitor screeched. Startled, he stood. Nurses barged into the room, crash cart pushed to the side of the bed. Without thinking, he backed out of the way. *What was happening? Was Joe dying?*

Wendsler scrutinized the medical staff at work as he watched them place medicines in Joe's IV and a dark haired nurse hooked lines to his chest. "Clear!" someone yelled.

Death drew near. Wendsler slipped into the hallway; sweat beaded his forehead, and trickled down his temple.

Twenty minutes later the doctor walked out.

"We were able to save him, and his vitals are stable. He's holding his own for now."

Wendsler nodded. "Thanks, Doc. Do you think he'll come out of this?"

"It's possible; time will tell."

Wendsler stepped back inside the dark room. Monitors beeped and blinked. He took Joe's hand.

"Fight, Joe. Fight for Chase. He needs you for guidance."

Joe's hand trembled.

"I know you hear me, buddy. Hang on and fight."

Wendsler squeezed Joe's hand as he leaned over him. "I will be back soon." Then he turned and headed toward the doorway. A red-haired nurse looked up as Wendsler approached the nurse's station.

"May I help you?"

"Please call this number if Mr. Spirit Eyes wakes." He handed her the number scribbled on a torn piece of paper. "It's very important."

"Sure will."

He nodded his thanks, and turned down the hallway, where the smell of death lingered in his senses. He pushed the exit door, scooted outside and took a deep breath. The sunset floated across the dusty sky, leaving a sense of harmony which life demanded.

Life was full of surprises, twists, and turns. Wendsler thought of his brother and the things they missed since he has passed away. He would make it right with Chase. It was his one chance to prove to his brother that good could come out of bad, even when the odds are against it.

Wendsler walked swiftly to his truck. The thought of losing Chase from the secret he would reveal devastated him. He'd locked that secret away for so long, but it had been for the safety of Chase's own life. He prayed the Creator would guide him. Chase would be angry with his father, even though the decision to keep it from him was for the best.

He walked past several parked cars and noticed there was a truck in the parking lot that resembled the vehicle that nearly ran him off the road.

"Hmm, wonder if they are following me?"

The engine cranked and Wendsler pulled in into gear. The traffic on the 101 would be calmer now. The valley had really grown from the good old days. So much more traffic roamed the streets along with the violence.

The sun started to set as the day ended. *Would Chase hate us for keeping such a secret?*

His thoughts ended as he noticed a spider dangling from a web in front of his face. "Oh, my friend, so what news do you bring? You are the weaver. You know our fate. I must be patient with Chase once I tell him. This was his destiny and he will learn that in time. You've inspired me today, my friend, by showing your presence. I will be there for Chase and guide him."

The sunset faded into the sky. Wendsler drove silently. He pondered on the news he would reveal to his nephew and prayed for understanding. The news would be hard at first to accept and understand, but the ancestors would guide Wendsler's words.

Then out of nowhere, a truck pulls up behind him, driving at a high rate of speed.

"Here we go again..."

He gripped the steering wheel, anticipating their next move, when the truck raced around him.

He chuckled. "Well, I guess I was just going to slow for them."

Chapter 24

Chase searched the perimeter of the house as the first patrol units arrived. Officer Begay stared at Chase.

"Now they're after you."

Chase scratched his head and nodded. "Sure seems that way, but luckily the bone beads missed me."

"If they had hit you, you would be very sick right now. Show me the damage."

"Come in."

They walked through the screened porch. Chase stopped. A string of beads lay at his feet.

Chase bent with a gloved hand, and picked up the beads, noticing a note a few inches away. He picked it up and Officer Begay leaned in so he could read the words.

The crumpled, coffee stained paper, read, *"You know what we want... The amulet. It belongs to the powers of evil. Turn it over or death will reign."*

"Officer Begay, they used magazines to cut the words out. They're trying to confuse us, but it's not working."

"What amulet are they talking about?"

Chase looked flustered. "It's the power of good and evil. The Dream Catcher amulet."

"Where is this amulet? What does it look like?"

Chase pointed to the door. "Inside."

He pivoted to face Officer Begay. "I have the object. It's a round, black and turquoise amulet that has a dream catcher and a hawk flying through it. The opening to the spirit world gifted to me by my father."

Officer Begay nodded. "The killer wants the amulet to gain power so he can cause havoc for the rest of us. This amulet would lead to total devastation if it were to fall into the wrong hands."

Chase swallowed. "And the chaos would forever belong to our children. I must protect the amulet at all costs."

Officer Begay glanced around. Bone beads were scattered all over the living room.

"Chase, we must gather every bead."

"Okay, some are embedded in the walls."

Officer Begay studied Chase. "You're lucky they missed you. I think this was a warning."

"I know. Wait till Uncle Wendsler hears about this."

The screen door screeched. "Hear about what?"

Chase turned to face his uncle. "Bone beads. You were right. They tried to get me."

"I figured they would. That's why I called to warn you. Look what I found lying by your truck."

Chase stepped toward his uncle. "A black feather...means a warning or protection. Let's hope the latter."

Wendsler cleared his throat. "I would assume it's a warning."

Chase's jaw dropped. "Uncle, your head is bleeding."

"Oh, I am okay."

Officer Begay glanced over. "You have a pretty nasty bump there. What happened?"

"Somebody ran me off the road on my way to Phoenix."

"Did you report it?"

"The truck disappeared before I could look back."

"What type of truck? Did you see the driver or did you get the license?"

"Blue older model Ford or Chevy truck, front quarter panel was dented in. The driver was a male with dark hair. No plate was on the truck."

"Sounds like Sam Kee. He's been acting strangely for the past several months."

"I bet he's the one I saw with Ralan," Chase said.

As if summoned, Ralan appeared on the porch. Silence filled the room.

Chase's heart quickened. "Ralan." Chase headed toward the door. "Can I help you?"

Ralan rubbed the back of his neck. "Thought I would stop by and see how the hunt for Harmony is going."

Chase pointed a finger at Ralan. "You know where she is, so stop playing these games!"

A wide grin played across Ralan's face. He chuckled. "Oh, I'm sure she's having a real good time, wherever she is."

Chase swept his arm around Ralan's neck and their bodies thudded to the ground. "You're a liar! Where is she?"

Chase punched him. "Here, how's this fist for fun?"

Arms tightened around him and Wendsler pulled Chase off Ralan.

"Chase, stop. This only harms our defense."

"He knows something and he's pushing me to my limits."

Ralan pivoted on his feet, chin held high, and dusted his jeans. "Next time we meet I hope you have your emotions in control."

Chase lurched toward him, but Officer Begay grabbed his shoulders.

"Enough, Ralan. Leave now, or I'll arrest you."

Ralan snickered and jumped into his truck, "Bye now."

The truck spun out and sent a shower of dirt toward the sky.

"I want to kill him." Chase punched the screen.

"Calm down. He wants to instill evil in you. His purpose is to gain control over your thoughts. Don't allow it, Chase."

"Harmony is in danger."

"He knows she is your weak point. Practice inner control."

Chase inhaled, then let out a slow breath. "Have to take a walk to clear my head."

Wendsler nodded his understanding. Chase had a hot temper, and he'd lost it with Ralan's words. Exactly what Ralan wanted to be able to penetrate his mind.

✶✶✶✶✶

Fresh air relaxed Chase immediately. The hawk flying above him proved his strength. Chase reached into his pocket and pulled out sage.

He bent down on his knees, raising his arms to the sky, offered a prayer, and lit the sage with a match to send smoke to the heavens.

"Creator, I offer this sage to our ancestors. Please send the bad away from me. All negative thoughts must vanish. I pray for our people. Guide me to make the right choices. Amen."

The smoke from the sage lingered in the area as it surrounded Chase. A sensation of peace and beauty lifted his spirits. Chase closed his eyes as an ancestor spirit evolved from the smoke and spoke to him. Chase's heart quickened as he noted that it was his father.

"My son, protect the amulet at all cost. There are two of these precious stones. Protect the one you have, and the other one will find its way into your hands soon. If the amulet falls into the wrong hands, complete destruction of our people is eminent."

"Father, it's you in spirit. I miss you so much. Please tell me what to do."

The misty spirit floated above. "I cannot change your destiny. This is all I can provide. I am always with you, my son."

The ethereal figure disappeared and Chase opened his eyes.

"Another amulet, I must tell Uncle Wendsler."

Chase strode a few yards behind his uncle's house. He stopped and glanced around the area. The house sat next to one of the most sacred sites on the reservation. It amazed Chase that his family had been given the land by a medicine man so long ago.

Another amulet meant twice the danger. Chase's heart quickened. "Please guide me to find it before Ralan does."

Chase knew his goal. Protect the amulet...protect the people... and find Harmony.

Chapter 25

Chase slammed the screen door as he came in.

"Uncle, I had a spiritual visitor. There's a second amulet, and we must find it as soon as possible."

"Your father visited you today. This second amulet is the twin to the first. Your father knows the power it holds."

Chase fumbled for words, "Then why does he not tell me where it is?"

"It's not for him to decide. It would change your destiny."

"Uncle Wendsler, is this what caused his death? The amulet....?"

Wendsler tapped his finger on his coffee cup. "You should know the truth. Come and sit down, for we have much to discuss."

Chase fingered the choker hanging around his neck as goosebumps formed on his arms.

"Son, this won't be easy for you to hear. Your father was the keeper of the amulet. To become the keeper, you must become a powerful shapeshifter and merge into other realms. Your father accepted the role proudly, but it meant keeping secrets from his family. Not doing so could mean death for all of us." He paused. "There are many more secrets that must be revealed to you. Patience, my son. Walk proudly in the knowledge."

Chase swallowed hard. "Why is it so dangerous?"

Wendsler sipped his coffee. "The amulet bundle came from the spirit world. The good spirits gave it to your father to protect. The evil spirits dwell on the possession of it. Now evil wants war with the good, because the amulet's power transferred into this realm now means more power. The keeper has powers like no other, but they can only be used if the spirits allow. Your father died fighting the evil shapeshifters and went alone into the cave without the amulet in his possession to protect him. The reason, to protect you."

Wendsler stepped to the window, shifting his eyes to the amethyst sky. "He gave the amulets to me. He said if anything happens to him to pass the amulets on to you once you were a man."

Chase rubbed his chin. "But why kill him?"

"I really don't know what took place that day. We believe it was to gain the possession of the amulets."

Chase locked eyes with his uncle. "I swear, I will find out why my father was murdered. He was a good man."

Wendsler wiped the tears from his face. "That he was."

"Uncle, I'm sorry for keeping my distance from you over the years. I felt you were connected to my father's death, but now I understand."

"Chase, thank you. I wanted this day to come where we could make amends, but unfortunately, the murders have caused so much harm to our people."

"Uncle, we will prevail. Dream Catcher came to us as a guide from the spirit world. There are more secrets, aren't there?"

Silence fell as the bronze sun set in the sky. Chase wondered what other reflections of his life would be divulged. And was he prepared?

$$*****$$

Harmony sat idle. The moment would come and she would be free. She searched through her hair. *Where are my hairpins? I know I had some in my hair before they took me.* Her fingers trembled searching for her needed weapon. *There's one.* She waited patiently until the moment would arrive and she could use the hairpin to pick the lock and set herself free. Once evil left, she would make her escape. The thought of being in Navajo land sent a streak of fear through her because she did not know the area, but her will was stronger than any fear.

Finally, Sam came to bring her dinner. "Here you go, eat up."

"Sam, you're a good man. Please reconsider helping me."

"Harmony, this is a tough decision for me. I have to stay true to my cause."

"There are other ways."

Sam cleared his throat. "You don't understand. You need power to do the things that make a difference. Ralan is the power that I need, and my life will finally get better."

Harmony sighed. "Ralan is a symbol of blackness and he is only looking out for himself. Once he has the amulet he will discard you like a tick."

Sam clenched his teeth. "Shut up. Ralan keeps his word. You will say anything to try to get me to help you. It will get you nowhere with me. Soon you will be his woman and then you'll understand our stance on this."

"That's where you're wrong, creep. I misjudged you. You're as sick as he is."

Sam paced. "Oh, the satisfaction on my face when I get to finish you off cause I know you will never become one with Ralan. I'll show no mercy."

Harmony's voice choked with tears. "Sam, you speak with a crooked tongue."

The pain reached deep into her stomach. The ache brought bile into her mouth. She swallowed it down.

She turned her back to Sam praying he would leave. The scuffling of feet assured her that he was.

＊＊＊＊＊

Darkness crept upon Mother Earth in unsettled silence. Harmony's hands were sweaty. Emptiness settled in the pit of her stomach. The desire to flee consumed her. The chance arrived for her escape. Her hand trembled as she attempted to unlatch the lock. She dropped the hairpin and it tumbled to the dirt floor. *Oh, I must hurry. Sam could return.* Fumbling through her hair, she found another pin. *Easy does it Harmony. You can do this.* The lock snapped and she turned it and the door flung open. The jump to safety could mean she could get hurt because the leap revealed was about ten feet to set her free.

"Control yourself. You must do this." Beads of sweat pelted her forehead. She took a deep breath and leaped out of the cage.

As her feet made contact with the dirt floor, pain penetrated her ankle.

Harmony grabbed it. "Oh great, now I'm hurt."

Darkness devoured the cave. "I have to go."

She limped across the dirt, trying to squelch her screams. "Creator, please don't let my ankle be broken. Keep me strong."

Hobbling, she felt her way with the palms of her hands against the earthen walls. The entrance was just up ahead.

Escape...Must go on. Chase... The lanterns at the entrance to the cave lit the way to freedom. Usually one of the posse members hung around outside, but tonight they weren't there. She could hear Ralan instructing Sam where to meet for their secret meeting.

Escape excited her. When Sam returned, the look on his face would be pure delight to see. But she would not be here to witness it. She crouched low at every noise. Then the awesome sight of the moon brought tears to her eyes.

Crickets sang loudly as she made her way out of the cave.

"Which way do I go? I must believe in my choices and myself. The moon and stars are my guides." The pale orb danced toward the west so that would be the direction to follow. With a quick, erratic pace, she trudged on. Doubt filled her thoughts. "Am I going the right way? Was I deluded, thinking I could escape on my own?"

The night sounds escalated her fear. The owl and the coyote were in full force tonight. The hoot from the owl was the sign of evil to come, and the coyote was the trickster, prone to trick its prey.

Harmony limped through the high mountain ranges. "I hope to find shelter of some sort soon. My ankle is really hurting and I need daylight to find my way."

Abruptly stopping, she glanced in all directions. "Creator, please protect me, and let me find refuge soon. My heart is strong but my body is weak from this ordeal."

The pace between her and danger grew larger. Soon, she prayed, help would find her before the evil hands of Ralan could.

Chapter 26

Chase sipped coffee, as he watched his uncle wring his hands.

Wendsler turned to face his nephew, the same deep-set eyes, the same straight nose, only the small birthmark on his neck setting them apart from his brother. "Chase, this is what's going to hurt the most." He paused, then plunged in. "Chase, another holds the amulet. One you do not know of, but one who is your brother. A brother who shares the same blood. Your twin."

Chase's loud voice echoed, eyes widening. "What! Are you kidding? A twin brother! Where? I can't believe nobody ever told me!"

Wendsler approached him as Chase turned his back to him.

"Please let me explain. It's complicated."

"How the hell has this been kept from me for so long?"

Wendsler fidgeted with his shirt collar. "We had to protect you both. The only way to do that was by separating you at birth. Don't judge until you know the story."

Chase paced, shaking his head. "To protect us from what? I don't understand. Are there evil forces after my family that I know nothing about?"

Wendsler nodded. "I know it's hard to understand. Let me explain."

Chase's heart pounded. "I'm waiting," he said.

"When you were born your father held both amulets. He was the only medicine man with the power to do so. He decided that he didn't want you or your brother to have to deal with what would come until you were grown." Wendsler ran his hands through his hair. "Your father contacted our ancestors from the spirit world for guidance. Evil wanted his powers, but to get the powers a person would have to kill him, take the amulets from his dead body, and kill both of you. Otherwise, you and your brother would hold the power."

Chase rocked on his feet. "Where is he? Where is my brother?"

"Come, it's time for you to meet him."

They walked to the barn in silence. The disbelief of the news of having a twin was almost overwhelming.

"Saddle Dream Catcher. He will lead us."

Chase hoisted the saddle onto the horse. "Hey there, boy," he said, and gently put the saddle across Dream Catcher. "I hope he is as honest and determined as I have been raised."

Wendsler guided Spirit, his horse, out of the barn. "It will take us half a day to get to him. His name is Trace."

The cool evening air drifted across the mountains. Chase welcomed it. A chance to reflect on having a twin brother.

"Uncle, does he know about me?"

"Yes, I told him about you six months ago."

"Did he not want to meet me?"

"He did, but I explained the importance of the situation and that you were not ready yet. Since they took Harmony, it prepared you for the evil that you will face."

Chase clenched his fist. "Harmony better be okay. She has nothing to do with this."

"Trust me, they will not harm her for fear of losing it all. They will use her as a bargaining tool. With Trace helping us now, we'll be ahead of the game. You're wearing your amulet, correct?"

"Of course, I always do."

Chase sat high on Dream Catcher, as the horse trotted through the brush. Ahead, Wendsler sat proud on Spirit, Chase wondered how his twin would accept him.

Silence fell between them. Only darkness remained, consuming Chase.

✶✶✶✶✶

Harmony crept alongside the towering mountains, twitches in her stomach. Her dusty hands clung to the hard surface as she crawled low to the ground. Trickles of blood escaped from under her nails.

In the distance, she saw a small cabin; there were lights on. "I must be careful. It could be evil lurking behind those walls."

She walked until she got close to the house; then she went down on all fours. She crawled on her hands and knees to the side of the porch, pulling herself up to take a glance inside. Her eyes widened as she noticed who was there. Chase was standing in front of the stove, cooking. She jumped to her feet and dashed onto the porch, swinging the door open.

"Chase! How I have wanted to see you!" she cried, wrapping her arms around his neck.

To her astonishment, Chase pulled away, "my name is Trace Spirit Walker," he said gently. "You must be Harmony."

She gasped and stepped back. "You look exactly like Chase!"

Trace chuckled. "He's my twin brother"

Harmony's stomach fluttered. "How can that be? He never mentioned you."

"He never knew I existed until just now. You will be safe here. Uncle Wendsler told me about you and Chase. I'm going to meet my brother for the first time soon."

Harmony sat in a wooden chair with a soft leather back. "Sorry but I'm shocked and confused. Why would he not know about you?"

Trace continued cooking. "It will make sense as soon as they get here."

"Chase is on his way here? I have evil people after me and I must warn him because he's the one they want to hurt."

Trace sniffed the air. The aroma from the acorn stew cast its spell. "Trust me, Chase will know what to do. Uncle Wendsler told me how he is, and I know he can conquer anything."

Harmony inquired further. "Did your brother know you existed? I mean, it's been a long time, and I don't understand."

"No, I learned about him from my Uncle Wendsler. Everything's going to be okay, Harmony. Our father left us as the keepers of the Dream Catcher amulet, so we are the Guardians of the Dream Catcher. This is what Ralan wants. It holds the power to the past, and the future of our people. If it were to fall into the wrong hands then evil would prevail and take over our reservations."

"So, does this have something to do with why your father was murdered?"

Trace's eyes widened. "Yes. Our father proved how important this is to our people and to me and my brother. He paid the ultimate price, his life, to protect us all."

Harmony eyes swelled with tears. "I'm so sorry, and I know that this is going to hurt Chase so bad."

The room filled with silence as the aroma of acorn stew spiraled around the room. Harmony's stomach growled but her heart was broken for Chase.

*****

"Uncle Wendsler, how much farther?"

"We are close."

The moon crested on the horizon. The animals crept around the desert, making their home in a barren place that was home to the Navajo and Apaches. The sense of the unknown swept through Chase's mind. *"Is it true? A twin brother."* The mere thought of him warmed his insides. He'd sensed all along that he was bonded to someone, and now he knew it was his brother.

As darkness swept over the land, the flicker of light caught his attention.

"Chase, we are here. Remember to take it slow and don't expect Trace to have all the answers. He's as confused as you are. Give him time and space."

Chase nodded. "I know, Uncle."

The horses whimpered. "It's okay, boy," Chase said softly to Dream Catcher. He swung his foot over the saddle. The mud stuck to his boots.

All at once, the door flung opened. "Chase, oh, Chase!"

Chase stopped in his footsteps. "Harmony!"

"I'm okay. Thinking of you and our love kept me strong."

Chase slipped across the ground. His arms grew limp, caressing her face. "Are you okay? Did they harm you in any way?"

"I'm okay now. Your twin brother is waiting inside."

144

"I know he is, and I can't wait to meet him. You can't imagine how thankful I am that you're here and safe. I'm sorry I couldn't find you. Ralan prevented me in so many ways, but I knew you would be okay."

"I managed to get free and wondered here. I saw Trace and thought it was you."

Chase glanced up, and there was his brother. "Trace," he said.

His twin stood on the porch, the spitting image of himself.

"My brother."

They embraced, and a sense of complete knowing ensued, a circle closing about them.

"I could not wait to meet you. Strange circumstances, but yet we are here, and I am thankful."

Trace leaned back. "Yes, brother, we have a lot to talk about."

"A lot to learn too."

The screen door screeched open. The faint breeze of acorn stew simmering drifted toward their noses. "Maybe we should eat first," Trace said with a gentle laugh.

Chase followed his brother into his house with a floating sensation, as if all his burdens had been lifted. He felt an overwhelming sense of pride and determination. A strong awareness of his own heartbeat awoke a deep, long sought for feeling of happiness.

~Chapter 27~

The teardrop-shaped table provided a place to sit and eat. Some felt it was a place to sit and filter the mind, sifting through the jumble of thoughts and feelings.

"Harmony, we need you to try and remember everything you can about where they held you."

Harmony blinked at Wendsler. "I believe it's about two miles south of here."

"The area of Canyon de Chelly." Trace swallowed as the words slipped through his bites of acorn stew.

Chase glanced up from his bowl. "Trace, do you know the area pretty good?"

"Yes, bro, very well. The caves there are sacred, and must be treated as so. They're trying to use the power of our ancestors to defeat us."

Wendsler stood, grasped his cup of coffee, and stared out the window, searching for answers to the chaos.

"Your thoughts, Uncle?"

"I feel a sense of dread. Unsure of this feeling, but I know it's nothing good."

Chase rose abruptly. "Uncle, we will defeat this evil. Nobody can withstand our power. We just have to believe in our ancestors and in the spirit world to guide us."

Wendsler pulled the handle on the screen door and with heavy footsteps, he stepped outside." Creator, guide these two brothers into the path of their ancestors. The evil is stalking us, and we must have a way to defeat it and bring peace back to our world."

Wendsler gazed to the sky with hope and faith on his side. He felt the quiet of the house and wondered what his nephews were up to.

* * * * *

A dignified silence engulfed the room.

"Trace, we must go into the nearest cave and practice. We must open the door to the spirit world by using our dream catcher amulets with each of our animal signs."

"Yes, brother, we shall go now if you would like."

Harmony gathered the dishes as she watched the man she loved prepare for the fight of his life and the life of so many of their people. Her heart felt pain and anxiety, but she had to show positive thoughts to Chase. She smiled. "Be careful and know our ancestors are walking with you."

Chase leaned into the screen. "Harmony, pray for us. I love you."

Chase turned and noticed Harmony's broad smile covering her face, but she couldn't hide the sadness that betrayed the panic she was feeling.

"Don't worry, honey. We will return. Everything will be okay. I'm thankful no harm came to you."

She smiled, shoulders out, and chin high. "I know you will win this battle."

Chase faced his brother. "Let's ride. We have a long fight ahead of us."

Chase waved at his uncle as they rode off. A sense of dread enveloped Wendsler's face. Chase would win this fight and prove to his uncle that he was the warrior that his father had taught him to be. And now he had an ally by his side.

*****

A cluster of red rocks scattered skyward. It disguised the ceaseless sun and the rusty sand cushioned the horses' footsteps.

"Not much farther."

Chase cupped his eyes, staring up at the sky. "A hawk...this is a sign from our grandfathers."

Trace picked up his pace. "We must arrive before the sun completely sets."

The horses' hooves pounded the brown, sandy dust. Time ticked holding the fate of their people.

The canyon walls towered in and out like a jigsaw puzzle, at times confusing.

"Chase, here is the cave."

They climbed off their horses and guided them inside the concave walls. Darkness spiraled around them.

"Trace, this is the spot."

"Let's try and open the portal to our ancestors. Since this is first time, we must concentrate and give full credit to our people."

Chase held his amulet out and touched it to Trace's. They were identical, except one had a hawk, the other a wolf.

"We come as one with our powers to protect our people from the wicked ways of this world. Please give sanctuary to our people and guide us to the deliverance of evil."

Without warning, the present became the past. A flashing, fluorescent light flickered around them.

"Chase, there is our father! Come on!"

Their feet landed on the ground like a slab of cinder blocks.

"Trace, we must focus!"

The wind swirled around them in pelting gusts, then died as if the source had been shut off, and all was calm.

Chase opened his eyes. The fresh mountain air felt so clean. The area felt different in some ineffable way. The landscape seemed untouched by humans.

"Trace!"

"I'm here."

The tranquility turned to disbelief, as time warped and carried them backward. The mountains towered around them where in their present world the mountains were smaller.

"Trace, we must find Father and seek his guidance."

"Let's walk, we will find him."

The walk seemed endless. Then the savory aroma of bacon penetrated their nose. The view of a strong man seized the moment.

"It's Father."

The image flickered, almost opaque, but it was their father. Tears streaked down their cheeks as their father spoke to them. "My sons. You have united. This is the cave where I lost my life. I'm sorry for not being there for you and that your lives changed because of my decision to separate you at birth, but it was for the greater good. The amulets hold strong, special powers. If they fall into the wrong hands then we, as a tribe, are doomed."

"Father, tell us what we must do." Chase pursed his lips.

"Son, the evil on the reservation must be eliminated. You have the power to do so, but use caution. These powers are strong and must be handled with caution. Look at the situation with a good heart. Time travel will make you weak, but I am your guide, and together the three of us will win. You must find the dream catcher that the evil witches are using and destroy it. Then the power of its holder will be defeated once and for all."

A layer of light filtered through but they listened closely to their father as he continued. "This evil of shapeshifting and murder will always reign, but we as guardians of the dream catcher can stop it. Dark beings use the power of the dream catcher to their advantage. Go and do as I say; then and only then can we stop the wicked ways that plague this land."

Bolts of light cascaded around them, striking the mountains. Then out of nowhere, they were back in the present world, which they had left for only a brief moment.

"Come on, Trace. We can't waste any time."

They turned the horses back and headed home. Soon, they would encounter the worst of evils.

Chase kept his thoughts to a minimum. He needed to focus on the truths his Father had uttered. A clear mind would be necessary in this battle.

"Trace, remember Father's words. We must keep our minds from clutter."

"I know. We can do this. I am glad you're here."

"As I am glad you are, brother. We have a strong connection that nobody can break. We must rely on our bond, as twins, to accomplish what we're meant to do."

Silence fell between the two brothers, but the close bond they shared revealed that their worlds entwined with each other... forever.

Chapter 28

The dream catcher hung to the cave wall as the feathers tumbled below, clinging to jagged rocks. He clasped his hands around it. Ralan stooped so he was eye to eye gawking at the dream catcher. "The amulet is all I need to gain complete power. I will rule soon and nobody will be able to stop me."

Silence captured Ralan's inner soul until the loud mutter of his friend took over. "Sir, the girl is gone."

Shades of achievement plastered Ralan's face. His plan had worked.

"Ahh, just as I planned. Now Chase will come after me and I will get the amulet."

Ralan clapped his hands tightly. "We must prepare. Get all the men together."

"I will become the poison of my people. Nobody will ever betray me again. My family's name will be idolized from the four sacred corners and beyond." Ralan's twisted grin transmitted secret knowledge. "Chase Spirit Walker has no idea what or who he's up against."

To savor the moment, he closed his eyes; only the sound of envy adhered to his thoughts. Power enveloped him and there was nothing that could stop the malevolence that surged inside him.

⁂ ⁂ ⁂ ⁂ ⁂

"Come, on boy, let's go." Chase pushed Dream Catcher to get back to Trace's house.

"We must speak to Uncle Wendsler, then we have to leave soon. Ralan and his clan are close to figuring out what he needs to gain his power."

Trace's horse galloped behind Chase. "I know, Brother. Good must prevail."

The mountains shrank into tiny obstacles as they made their way back to the house. Soon evil would make its stand and they were both ready.

✶✶✶✶✶

Wendsler lifted the cup of coffee to his lips, staring out into the world of discontent. "We must win this battle, Great Spirit. Without our world protected, we will cease to exist. I know my nephews can do this, but at what cost? I pray for knowledge and the strength to help them. *Nizhi bee tsodiszin*, in your name I pray, *táá ákótée doo*, Amen."

The rocking chair squeaked as Wendsler sat to pray for guidance. Soon the battle would be on and he would open his heart to *Diyin Ayoo At eii*, God, our Supreme Being and giver of life, and the mountain spirits to guide and win this fight.

The sun set in the western sky as the sound of hooves pounded along the dirt pathway.

"Chase, have you learned the path to defeat this evil?"

Chase jumped off his horse and eyed Wendsler. "Uncle, of course I have. We will win this fight. I need some herbs from the garden. Did Trace plant any?"

"Sure, I did. It's over there behind the house near the creek."

"Chase, I will gather what you need as you and Trace prepare inside. What else do you need?"

"Thank you, Uncle. I'll need wolfsbane, foxglove, dragon's blood, and moonflower."

"I'll have it ready for you soon."

Chase stepped onto on the porch, the screen door creaking as he opened it.

"Harmony, we have to go soon. Can you please try and remember which way you came from?"

"Chase, I broke limbs as I walked. I wanted to make sure I didn't go in a circle and return back to my captors."

"Okay, my love. We'll rest for a while, but at nightfall we'll ride out." Chase turned to Trace. "My brother, we must rest. Then we will seek revenge for our father and for the innocent medicine men who are dying at the hands of Ralan."

"Sure, Brother, we'll attack under the moonlight.

Chase walked to the makeshift bed near the door. He laid his head down, facing the door. He wondered what would happen if they were defeated. Heaviness crept to his eyes, forcing them shut, when suddenly a bright light forced Chase to cover his eyes. *"What is going on?"*

A blast of colors reflected a man standing in the traditional clothing of their people. *"Doklini, is that you?* The most revered medicine man of the 1800s stood before Chase to offer guidance.

"Son, it is I, *Doklini*. You must attack the enemy by the light of the Apache Moon. We know if one of our warriors dies, they will meet the same conditions in the spirit world, as they will leave in this one. This is very important. Never give up and walk in the spirit of Cochise and Geronimo. Remember the Ghost Dance. It will all make sense when you are in battle. These words must be in your mind when you are in doubt. You have Chiricahua blood and it will be revealed tonight. My spirit is always with you."

A flash of light and a hawk swooped down and touched Chase, which startled him awake.

Chase's head beaded with sweat. *"Usen*, our Supreme Being and giver of life, protect us in this war we are about to encounter."

Sleep fell heavy upon Chase as his eyes closed once more, *"Only Usen can protect us now."*

*****

Night approached. Chase prepared his inner being. *"I am ready and I have Usen and my ancestors with me."*

"Son, come outside. There are special visitors here to see you.

Chase looked bewildered, but followed his uncle. The full moon spewed on the beauty before his eyes.

"Our mountain spirit dancers came before our battle to offer their protection and guidance."

The masked spirit dancers stood adorned in their clothed masks. Their crowns, worn on the top of their heads, made out of wood with tall, pointed ends, were brightly painted.

"Come, Chase, we must sit around the fire as our spirit dancers perform the protection dance. "Trace followed his brother and sat in front of the fire. They crossed their legs and listened to the drums beat, spreading calm over the listeners.

The mountain spirit dancers moved to the beat of the drum, blessing the two men sitting in front of them, who had to face evil soon.

The dance ended and the dancers left as quietly and humble as they had arrived.

"Chase and Trace, please stand."

The two men quickly responded to their uncle.

"I place the feather of the hawk around you, Chase. *Usen*, God and our ancestors protect you. Your spirit amulet is the hawk. He is the messenger and he'll guide you. Your vision will be seen through your own eyes."

Wendsler turned to face Trace. He was so proud of these two brothers. "I place the fur from the wolf around you, Trace. *Usen*, God and our ancestors protect you. Your spirit animal is the wolf, which is the protector. Beware of the owl spirit, which will follow you closely. He is a bad sign and messenger of evil. Go in honor of our people and make us proud."

Wendsler pivoted and walked away. Tears trickled down his face for the love he held for these brave young warriors.

"Trace, we are ready. Let's go."

They mounted the horses and Chase turned to Harmony.

"We shall return. I love you."

Before Harmony could respond, the two brothers disappeared under the full moon, the Apache moon.

*****

They approached the cave where Ralan sat waiting. The branches Harmony broke off led them to the exact cave.

Thoughts of Harmony entered his mind. He had not hugged or kissed her but he thought it would be easier for her, not to witness the strength of his emotions. He hoped she realized that.

"Trace, we must smudge ourselves in corn pollen before we continue."

They faced each other and sprinkled corn pollen on themselves as Chase lead the prayer. "*Usen*, God, please protect and guide us in what we must accomplish today. Take our hearts and weld them together so we shall overcome this dark force."

Then Chase sprinkled the pollen in the four sacred directions. Turning to his brother, he instructed. "Trace, we must walk in from here. Keep in the shadows with the full moon protecting us."

Trace nodded, and they dismounted, as Chase slapped the horses rump to scatter them in the opposite direction so they would not be seen.

The dust slid across their boots, as they crawled on hands and knees to get close to the cave entrance.

Chase pointed to the two men standing guard at the entrance. The entrance to the cave was transformed by the light of the moon, sending ripples across the entrance.

Abruptly, they faced each other. "Did you hear that? It sounded like rocks moving. You go around that way and I will head this way. Check out everything. Leave nothing unturned. Tonight is an important night to Ralan. We must make sure it happens as planned.

Trace noticed that one of their horses was in the area and had tripped on a rock. Trace circled around to the other side in hopes that he could scare the horse away.

"No, Trace!"

Out of nowhere, Chase watched as two men grabbed his twin.

"Damn it!"

Chase leaned against the red, protruding rocks.

"Now what the hell do I do?"

Without warning, Ralan appeared. His hair tasseled and clothes filthy.

"Now, Chase, we know you're out there. Wow, you have a twin brother. Come on out or he will die."

Chase circled back around the cave. *There has to be another entrance.*

He reached out and laid his hand against the outer wall of the cave. The opening surfaced. "Hell, yes."

His uncle was right. His eyes would serve him well.

Chase climbed through the opening and made his way through a small, narrow space. Four men stood in a circle, talking, Trace tied to the wall.

Chase realized it was time to shape shift. He closed his eyes, placed his hand on the hawk amulet. He concentrated on his brother, on Harmony, and on his people, transforming him into the hawk.

He flew out of the small opening and made his way to Ralan's dream catcher. It must be destroyed but he had to hide it until he could free Trace. It would take both of them.

He picked it up with his beak and flew it into the small opening. Now he must free Trace. He swooped down behind the four men, and landed on his brother.

Trace glanced up as the piercing eyes of the hawk landed on the ledge, and watched in shock as the hawk's beak picked up his wolf amulet and turned him into his spiritual animal...the wolf.

The wolf snarled.

"Look, it's a wolf, run."

Chase flew off toward the opening as Trace ran toward the group of men. As he approached, three of them ran down the long cave wall to get out.

Ralan touched his amulet and turned into the owl. He swooped down and attacked Trace. Quickly, Chase flew out of the opening and straight at Ralan. Trace tackled Ralan's winged body. The ripping and tearing of the owl brought Ralan back to his normal form. Chase and Trace quickly returned to their human forms and took the dream catcher apart, releasing the evil spirits. They stood over Ralan... dead.

Lights flickered throughout the cave. Without warning, Chase's father appeared with Geronimo by his side.

"My sons, I'm proud of you. Both of you are now the guardians of the dream catcher. Our great leader, Geronimo, came to speak to you."

Geronimo stood proudly, shoulders straight. "Guardians of the dream catcher, we are proud of you. From this point forward, both of you will watch over our people. Stand proud and always put them first."

Beams of light encircled the twins and a loud clash of thunder shuddered all around. Silence ensued.

Chase opened his eyes. The battle was over for now.

"We won, Brother. The evil dispersed as we took the dream catcher apart and the vileness died with it. Father and our great leader Geronimo are proud, and we're guardians of the dream catcher for our people."

"I'm grateful. We must offer thanks to our ancestors now."

Chase turned to thank the spirits. Trace followed suit. Chase's heart beat proudly with his father and Geronimo having appeared.

"*Usen*, thank you for allowing good to win over the wicked that has plagued our reservations. My people are thankful and we shall forever protect Mother Earth from the wrongs brought forth by man. *Ahehye'e.*"

Chapter 29

~One Month Later~

Harmony stood beside Chase as they waited for Wendsler to head to Oak Flats.

"Glad Joe came out of that coma."

Wendsler stood on the porch. "How did he take it about his son?"

Harmony glanced up. "He took it pretty hard. I told him I was here if he needs me. I have to pick him up from the hospital tomorrow. He can't wait to get back home. He talked about when he was in a coma he could see his team members putting out the forest fire. He discussed how when he was a young man, his desire was to become one of the best at fighting forest fires, and he had achieved that by becoming a Geronimo Hot Shot. He said they are the best. His many years as a Geronimo Hot Shot had filled his life, since the passing of his wife. He talked about how their only son, Ralan, had been in and out of drug rehab for several years since Judi's death, but he'd finally made something of himself and now he was dead. I felt so sorry for him when he teared up and explained how Ralan had gone to school to become a vet and a horse trainer and he had been earning respect in his field. He said he'd been very proud of his son, then it turned out he was the evil that walked the reservation. Very hard to hear this coming from our elder, but he will be okay."

Chase glanced at Harmony and he could see the pain on her face. To her, Joe was more like a dad so he changed the subject.

"Sweetheart, should we tell them the news?"

Harmony smiled as Trace spoke up, tilting his head to the side. "So what's the news, are you moving back there with Joe?"

Harmony gazed at Chase. "Well, my brother, we have better news than that. I've asked Harmony to marry me. She has accepted."

Trace chuckled. "I thought you two were up to something. I'm so happy for you."

"Trace, will you be my best man?"

"Of course, it would be my honor."

Chase turned to his Uncle as Harmony approached him." Would you give me away?"

Wendsler teared up. "It would be my honor."

"So when is the big date?"

Chase smiled. "Sometime in the next six months."

"Well, we best get to planning it. Now, let's head to Oak Flats."

"Oh, by the way, we plan it to be performed at Oak Flats, even though we're fighting against the mining companies."

Wendsler stood proud. "Perfect place, now let's head that way and see what destruction they have done."

They sat in silence as they headed down Highway Sixty into Superior. Oak Flats is sacred to the Apache and now the mines were trying to take control of it.

*****

Chase stood at the foot of Oak Flats, Harmony by his side. In the distance, Apache Leap stood strong.

The tall steel shaft rose toward the sky. It looked like a cage and was used to transport people and equipment underground.

"The next battle stands before us, Trace. The mine companies will try to take our religious rights. We must not let this happen."

Wendsler stepped forth. "They will not take this sacred land. This is where our future children will hold their ceremonies."

Chase placed his hand on his uncle's shoulders. "We will fight to protect this sacred land. We'll make a stand."

The hawk soared above. Its wings spanned out and it let out a fierce scream. "The hawk is the messenger from the spirit world. He will guide us, Uncle. He'll never let us down."

Wendsler turned and walked to his truck as the mineshaft started up its daily workload. The roaring of the motors echoed throughout the site. The humming of drilling drained out all the beautiful songs the birds in nearby trees had sung before. The animals were starting to disappear.

"Trace, Wendsler is very concerned and his heart is troubled. We must be observant to the feelings he's revealing to us. We must defeat this new evil. The spirits of Apache Leap are disturbed. They will never permit the desecration of this holy land. We have another war ahead of us."

"I know, Chase. We have a connection to the spirit world. We will prevent this. Our ancestors are with us and will guide our spiritual beings in the right direction."

Harmony shook her head. "I have been covering this in the paper, and the mines have the power and the money."

Chase tensed. "We, as Apache People, have the right to this land. Life has been hard for all of us, and now the mines and the government must stop. We must stop them."

Trace nodded. "I stand with you, and I'll give everything inside of me to stop it. There's been enough death on this land."

Chase's brow furrowed. "This I know too well. Our ancestors had a secret path that led up to Apache Leap. They were attacked in the early morning hours and a lot of them died. The remainder ran toward the west end of the mountain, where they leaped to their deaths. This site will be protected because we hold our sacred ceremonies there; our sweat lodge is there. It breaks my heart that we must always defend what is holy to us."

Trace's tightened his fists. "I'm with you, Bro."

Harmony's radiant glow blossomed. "Chase, don't worry. You are kind and a plan to defeat this will come to you. You're the leader of our people, our future medicine man."

Chase raised his eyebrows and offered her a questioning gaze. "I hope I'm strong enough, honey. I'll do my best."

Chase took Harmony's hand, walked down the dirt road, and climbed into the truck. Silence enveloped them. Highway 60 revealed the sacred land all around them. The protruding mountains teetered around the heartbreak of the Apache people.

Chase peered out his window, taking in the beauty of this sacred landscape.

"I will do everything in my power to protect our sacred land. I just pray death will not occur in the process. My stance remains

forever. Oak Flats will not be taken from my people," he vowed.

The roar of the truck engine brought Chase back to reality. In the distance, the first signs of mining held his eye. The steel shaft stood erect. His heart felt heavy.

The fight was on for Oak Flats and Apache Leap. He would stand his ground for this holy land. What would come of it? Only time would tell, but he would give his life for the area and his people. Soon he was afraid that could turn to a possibility.

The evil of Ralan had ended and Joe Spirit Eyes had recovered and was now one of his mentors. Joe had a sad heart because his son, but was a strong medicine man. He would heal in time.

Chase was happy, for his Uncle Wendsler had become one of his many teachers to learn the medicine way. Life was good for now. *Harmony accepted my proposal, and we will be married soon.*

Now the fight for our spiritual way of life and our holy lands was at the forefront. This was going to be a battle but not one he would lose.

"*Usen*, guide us on this new journey. Give us the wisdom to fight this."

Chase closed his eyes. The new challenge for his people was to protect what was sacred for the future generations of our children.

The children....Oak Flats and Apache Leap will be a part of our children's life. No matter what cost that had to be paid....even death!"

They headed home, each with a heavy heart. The ringing of Chase's cell phone brought him back to reality.

"This is Chase."

Silence ensued. Only getting part of the conversation was enough to send chills up Wendsler's spine.

"Copy. I, was just in the area of Oak Flats and the mind shaft, but I'll head back."

Chase hung up and turned to Trace. "Major accident. An employee, they believe, was pushed down the shaft and killed. I have to return to investigate."

"Why do they believe he was pushed?"

Chase cracked his knuckles. "That's the thing. He was there alone but they had cameras and it shows him being shoved by a spirit of our people dressed in late 1800s attire."

Harmony stared at Wendsler who remained quiet.

Wendsler rubbed the back of his neck as he turned the truck around.

"What is it, Uncle?"

"The spirits are angered. They've come to claim the land and will prevent any further desecration of the land. I warned the mine companies, but they'll have to learn the hard way."

Chase stared out of the window, fixing his eyes on the heavens. Was this the beginning of what was to come? Would our people be judged for the curse of destroying their sacred sites? How many lives would be lost before the mining companies listened to our voices? Already death reigned and nothing could stop it. The vengeance of their ancestors would prove that the sacred site should be left alone. But would the mine companies take heed, or meet their own demise?